THE BARON
AND
THE CHINESE PUZZLE

THE BARON
AND
THE CHINESE PUZZLE

by
JOHN CREASEY
as
ANTHONY MORTON

CHARLES SCRIBNER'S SONS

New York

CONTENTS

1

THE MANNERINGS TALK

"I SIMPLY don't believe it," Lorna Mannering said. "There's something you haven't told me."

"Not a thing," Mannering assured her. "You know just as much as I do." He smiled, half teasing. "All we have to decide is whether to go."

Lorna did not speak at once, and Mannering watched her. Slowly, his smile faded. There was so much that was precious and familiar about her, yet every time he studied her in this way he noticed something he had not really seen before; and that was remarkable after twenty years and more of married life. It was not simply that the years had given her beauty more maturity; the marvel was that her skin and her eyes had the bright freshness of youth. It was not just that she might concede a little to the latest fashion in lipstick or eye-shadow, the latest fad in shaping her eyebrows, or the latest hair-style. It was some feature, tiny though it might be, that he had never noticed.

At this moment, it was the tiniest mole a hair's breadth below her right eyebrow; one hair too many had been plucked, and so revealed it. Why should so trifling a thing bring this mood upon him? A mood both of humility and gratitude for their years together.

Lorna's lips moved; they were shapely and rather full. Mannering expected her to say whether she was satisfied with his assurance or not. Instead, she asked almost sharply:

"Why are you looking at me like that?"

He could not easily tell her the truth; so he hedged.

"Like what?"

"In that peculiar way—as if you'd never seen me before."

"Was I looking like that?" asked Mannering, intrigued.

7

"You know you were. John, you are keeping something back about this invitation to Hong Kong, aren't you?"

"No," he answered, positively. He was both glad and sorry that the moment had passed, because he could not really have put into words how he felt, how in those few seconds he had both yearned for her and realised how much she meant to him.

"Honestly?"

"Absolutely everything I know is in that letter," Mannering asserted. "Would you like to read it again?" Gradually he was beginning to think clearly, to remind himself that they had been talking about an invitation that they should go to Hong Kong a month from now to see a collection of Chinese antiques.

Lorna had taken the letter from the table in the small study in their Chelsea flat. It was evening in early January, the curtains were drawn, the flat was warm, the dark wood of the antiques in this small, pleasant room glowed in the subdued light. Lorna was sitting on a pouffe, facing Mannering, who sat in a winged armchair. On the table were two glasses.

Everything here was calm and pleasant, remote from the violence and the danger Mannering knew his wife so feared. He watched her as she read the letter again. There were a few flecks of grey in her almost black hair. Her complexion had hardly a blemish, but as she concentrated a furrow appeared between her brows, and she had an almost aloof expression; the few people who did not like her were prone to say that she had a touch of arrogance.

She looked up.

"Who is Raymond Li Chen?"

"A Hong Kong antique dealer."

"He can't simply want you to go to see the exhibition."

"If I know the business instincts of a Chinaman, he wants to say 'thank you' for past services so as to make sure I don't forget him in the future. Just that."

Lorna was half frowning when she said:

"I wish I knew whether to believe you or not. Have you done a lot of business with him?"

Mannering picked up his whisky and soda, sipped, and said:

"Over the years, a lot, yes. I buy ivory and jade from his catalogue, and recommend him to clients who are passing through Hong Kong." It was strange that he was in such a thoughtful and reflective mood tonight; he had not been when he had come home from his shop, Quinns, in Hart Row, Mayfair; in fact, he had been half excited at the thought of taking Lorna to the Far East. He should have realised that she would immediately begin to look for snags, but it had not occurred to him. They lived closely together, they had much more affinity than most married couples, and yet it still needed a conscious effort to make him see a situation as Lorna saw it.

"I haven't heard you talk about him," Lorna said.

"I dare say that we have a hundred customers whom I don't talk about."

"I suppose so," Lorna conceded, half dubiously. Then she laughed. "Sorry, darling. I didn't mean to sound as if I didn't believe you." She sipped her gin and French. "You haven't talked much about business at all, lately."

"There hasn't been much to talk about. If it comes to that . . ." He broke off.

"What were you going to say?"

"Forget it."

"I don't want to," Lorna said. "We haven't talked like this for a long time. Months. We should have, shouldn't we?"

After a pause, Mannering leaned forward and said quite simply:

"Yes, but I hadn't consciously felt anything was missing."

"What were you going to say?"

"That you haven't said much about your sitters and your painting lately."

"I haven't, have I? John . . ."

"Yes?"

"You know what we're saying, don't you?"

"What are we saying?"

9

After a much longer pause, and with almost too much emphasis, Lorna said:

"That we're growing apart."

Mannering would not have believed that anything could startle, even shock him, as much as that did. "*Growing apart*" echoed and re-echoed in his mind, and his first reaction was to reject it out of hand. His mood soon changed; in fact, as he forced himself to face up to the implication in the words, he could not reject them out of hand.

Lorna's lips were curved in a smile which did not touch her clear grey eyes. Mannering felt sure that she had startled herself quite as much as she had him. There was anxiety in the very way her broad forehead wrinkled, and the groove between her eyes deepened. It would be easy to imagine that she felt disturbed, if not alarmed.

"Did I really imply that?" asked Mannering quietly.

"The important thing is, did you mean it—do you think it?"

Mannering had never known such a moment with his wife; never known such tension between them. These weren't simply words spoken without thinking. They came out of the depths of their subconscious anxiety; uncertainty about the mood of their relationship had come, unbidden, to the surface of their minds.

"John," Lorna said, with a catch in her voice, "is that what you meant?"

Mannering put his glass down, slowly, and took her hands.

"No," he said.

"You're sure?"

"Positive."

"John," she repeated, almost inaudibly. "Don't lie to me. What were you thinking when you were looking at me just now? I want to know. I have to know." She let him take her hands but did not yield towards him; if anything it seemed to him that she was sitting more upright on the pouffe, straining away from him.

He made no effort to draw her closer.

10

"I wish I could tell you," he said.

"Of course you can tell me!"

"No, I can't. Not really."

"John," she said, and although it was subdued there was a note of near-panic in her voice. "You must tell me. I tell you I must know."

Very gently, Mannering smiled.

"Then I'll try. I think I was looking at you and trying to imagine how empty life would have been without you over the past twenty years. I simply couldn't imagine, I couldn't say that when you asked me, could I? But my sweet!"

Tears came as if from nowhere, spilling over her lashes and down her cheeks.

"I know I'm a fool," she managed to say at last, through the tears. "I know you'll laugh at me, but you gave me such a fright. I thought—— Oh, never mind what I thought!"

Mannering waited a few minutes, while she dabbed her eyes. Colour crept back into her cheeks, making them glow; she was very slightly olive-skinned, as if far back in her ancestry there had been Spanish or Italian blood. Sometimes she made him think of the Italy of the Middle Ages, the courts of the Borgias and the mediaeval popes. That was a fact, although he had never given it serious thought before. Over the carved oaken mantelpiece in this room was a picture of a smiling cavalier dressed in all his seventeenth-century furbelows—and with his, Mannering's, face. She saw him as from the past, too. And she had made him handsome enough to match her own beauty.

He poured her out another drink.

"You still haven't answered about Hong Kong," he reminded her.

"Is there time to go by sea?" asked Lorna.

He had not thought of it, but calculated swiftly.

"We-ll—if we get off early next week, yes, I should think so. I'm not sure about the sailing dates, but we can find out in the morning. Will you come if we can?"

"Yes," Lorna said, and went on in a positive tone: "I'll

11

come in any case. If we can share the same flat in our own home city and drift apart, I'd hate to think what would happen if we put half the world between us."

"You really did take that too seriously," Mannering said ruefully.

"I don't think I did, you know," Lorna smiled, and although this time her eyes were bright with laughter, too, they were also touched with seriousness. "You haven't talked half as much about business and Quinns as you used to, and I've hardly said a word about pictures and painting and exhibitions. So each of us must have made the other think that we weren't interested. John . . ."

"Hm—hm?"

"When were you last up in the studio?"

Her studio was in the attic here, not twenty seconds away. He had to think, and think hard before he answered.

"When the Penders were here."

"At the end of September."

"It can't be!" Mannering was shocked.

"But it was," insisted Lorna. "And I haven't set foot inside Quinns since the Legevre Exhibition, when I wanted to study that Legevre miniature." She glanced up at the portrait of him in fancy dress. "I know one thing."

"What's that?" Mannering asked.

"We'll have plenty to talk about when we're on the ship!"

They both laughed. Quite suddenly Lorna was on Mannering's lap. His arms were tight about her, and they were close together in a rebirth of excitement they had not known for a long time.

Mannering's lips were very close to Lorna's. "Sweet."

"Yes?"

"I've just thought of something else we've almost forgotten lately."

"What's that?"

He squeezed her even more tightly.

"*Think*," he urged.

*   *   *

12

It was a wonderful evening; a perfect evening; and when he lay in bed, half dozing, watching Lorna's profile against the pale light of the street lamps, and feeling the warmth of her bare shoulder against his, he thought:

"It's going to be a second honeymoon."

He smiled to himself, realising what his more cynical friends would think of that sentiment, even surprised at himself. He felt so right; contented was probably the better word.

Suddenly, Lorna spoke in a quiet voice: "Do you think anything will happen to spoil it?"

"I don't see why it should," Mannering replied. "I thought you were asleep. What made you say that?"

"I suppose because I suddenly felt frightened. It's almost too good to be true, to feel as I do now."

The strange thing was that he could not laugh her fears away. Nothing would make him admit it, but he half shared them.

"You're listening to the nonsense of ghosts," he said.

"I know," said Lorna. "I suppose we should wish that there were no ghosts, but I don't. I can't. If there had been no yesterday, how could there be today?" Suddenly, she was hugging him tightly, quite unmistakably fearful of those "ghosts" they would not name.

*   *   *

There were the vivid memories of the days before they had married, when Mannering had been the Raffles of his age, known as the Baron, a veritable Robin Hood robbing the rich to help the poor. Today, it was hardly possible to believe he had broken into houses, forced safes and strong-rooms, and tangled with the police. There were the ghosts of the shadows of the police, too, some of whom suspected John Mannering to be the Baron, even to this day. How was it possible to be sure that no one still cherished the hope of proving that, in court?

There were still nearer ghosts, the memories of criminal cases which he had investigated, often with the police—cases which had brought danger and near-death, with dismay and anxiety for Lorna. Yet there was a funny side to that, too; because of these cases the police had often turned to him for professional advice. He was a consultant to New Scotland Yard as an expert on precious stones and *objets d'art*. Nothing could have made him more respectable, or put a more righteous seal upon his reputation.

Soon he heard Lorna's even breathing, and was glad that she had fallen asleep. He was not at all sleepy. He kept trying to imagine any reason why Raymond Li Chen might be particularly anxious for him to visit Hong Kong.

Was it reasonable that he or anyone else should be invited to an exhibition ten thousand miles away, simply to look and admire? Was Lorna right?—as she had been often in the past —reading an ulterior if not sinister motive in something which he had taken at its face value?

He wondered if there was any way to find out.

2

THE MANNERINGS IN A HURRY

IT was one of those periods when the Mannerings were without a living-in maid, so they breakfasted in the kitchen, Lorna lightly, Mannering heartily. Both were bright-eyed, and talk flowed freely, with an underlying note of excitement.

"You're really serious, John?"

"I'm going to find out about the ships today."

"What will the weather be like?"

"In Hong Kong, lovely. Even the Red Sea shouldn't be too bad."

"How long can you stay away?"

"Five or six weeks—if we sail there and fly back that should give us plenty of time."

14

"I suppose so," Lorna said, half dubiously. "Supposing there isn't a ship?"

"There will be."

"But if there isn't . . ."

"We'll go as far as we can by ship. We can certainly get to Singapore, and fly on from there."

Fresh excitement made jewels out of Lorna's eyes.

"I'll need some clothes, and you'll hardly have time to breathe to get things arranged at the shop."

"I'll breathe," Mannering assured her. "Larraby might be a bit breathless, but—what's the time?"

"Just turned nine. Remember, we slept late!"

"I remember," Mannering said softly. "And I also remember why. With a bit of luck they should be open."

"Who should be?" demanded Lorna.

"Who but the ubiquitous Thomas Cook's," answered Mannering, and he stretched out for the telephone. Lorna sat motionless, giving the impression that she still was only half convinced.

The travel agency answered, and soon Mannering was talking to a man with a brisk voice and an encyclopaedic knowledge of passenger ships and sailings. Over the years this office had done so much work for John Mannering and his clients that they were almost friends.

"Yes, Mr. Mannering, and you may be lucky . . . for *Orienta* on Tuesday next." Mannering mouthed "Tuesday" to Lorna, who mouthed back "What?"

"The newest and undoubtedly the best ship in the P. & O. fleet, an improvement even on the *Canberra*. I was told only yesterday that she was fully booked. However there may be a cancellation, I heard a rumour that the High Commissioner for Malaya was likely to postpone his voyage. I will know in a few minutes. Shall I call you back?"

"When?" breathed Lorna.

"Tuesday," whispered Mannering.

"What was that, Mr. Mannering?"

"I stifled a sneeze," Mannering said.

15

Lorna was close behind him, arms round him; he could feel the soft pressure of her breasts against his back. He turned his face upwards, and the sight of the radiance in her eyes almost hurt.

"So we are going?"

"Did you ever doubt it?"

"Won't keep you a minute, Mr. Mannering, I'm calling P. & O. on the other line. Meanwhile, here are a few details of the ship and ports of call . . ."

"The extension!" Mannering hissed at Lorna, and she flew across the room towards the hall.

"This is a very bad line," the Cook's man complained. "I was saying, the *Orienta* is the newest ship in the fleet. It is diesel driven, forty-six thousand tons gross weight, one funnel aft. She has built-in stabilisers, of course, and is fully air-conditioned. The whole of the promenade and the sun deck are given over to First Class, but in Cabin there is plenty of deck accommodation——"

"Can you tell me the ports of call?" interrupted Mannering. He could see Lorna standing by the telephone in the hall, the receiver at her ear.

"By all means. First call is Aden, for twelve daylight hours, the next is Karachi, also for twelve daylight hours. Third is Bombay, two full days, next is Colombo, one day—no time to run up to Kandy, I fear. Fifth, Singapore, sixth Hong Kong— the ship goes on to Japan and then Australia and New Zealand, across the Pacific with the calls at Suva, Fiji——"

"I hate to say it," interrupted Mannering, "but Hong Kong is as far as we can hope to go."

"I quite understand," said the Cook's man. "Hold on, please."

They could hear him talking on the other line. Lorna hitched up a stool and sat down. Whatever fears she had felt the night had driven away, and she wanted nothing more than to go on this voyage. She called across:

"When does it reach Hong Kong?"

"Forgot to ask," Mannering called back.

16

"On the nineteenth day," answered the Cook's man, without warning. "Ha, ha, ha, you didn't realise I had a telephone to each ear, did you? ... Half a mo' ... Here we are!" The tone of his voice told of good news. "The High Commissioner is going after all, I'm told he's a very congenial companion, just married for the second time, you know. His first wife died of cancer. His new wife is quite young, but you don't want me to tell you all the gossip in advance, do you? There is a double cabin available on 'A' deck. It is not one of the best but has an excellent position amidships, close to the main hallway, beauty salon, stairs and lifts to the dining-room. The P. & O. had kept it back in case of a last minute emergency, and once I mentioned the name of Mr. Mannering it was pencilled in for you. Shall I confirm?"

"Yes, please," Mannering said.

"How much is it?" Lorna wanted to know.

"The fare per person double occupancy is £320 1s. exactly," the Cook's man said. "If you'll let me have the confirmation in writing, for formality's sake ..."

When they rang off, they walked towards each other and met in the middle of the hall. Strangely, they were not smiling; it was almost as if the ease of getting the accommodation was an anti-climax.

Lorna actually shivered; but a moment later, she laughed.

"We've only five days to get ready in, darling! No more lying in for you!"

* * *

Grey-haired, gentle-faced Larraby, manager of Quinns, seemed genuinely delighted. In the long, narrow shop which for nearly four centuries had contained the old and the gracious in furniture, jewels, and paintings as well as *objets d'art*, he smiled into Mannering's eyes. He was reflected in the burnished gold of a ceremonial tray from Bangkok, hanging on the plastered wall from a massive oak beam which was even older than the tray. Outside, London's traffic sped and roared and groaned within a few yards, but Hart Row itself had

17

recently become a paradise for pedestrians only; access for vehicles was at the back of the shop.

"I'm very glad indeed, Mr. Mannering, I've felt for some time that you needed a good holiday. You've been working very hard."

"Have I, Josh?" Mannering was vaguely surprised.

"Unnecessarily hard," Larraby assured him, with a faint note of reproof in his voice. "How long do you expect to be gone, sir?"

"Six weeks or so," Mannering answered.

"The season doesn't really begin until after Easter," mused Larraby. "You could quite comfortably extend the trip by two or three weeks if you wished."

He did not add "everything here will carry on as usual, you will hardly be missed", but his words implied it.

A little ruefully, Mannering settled down at his bow-fronted Queen Anne desk in a small, well-appointed office filled with antiques and small pieces of great intrinsic value. He wrote the confirmatory note to the travel agents, and went through a list of matters awaiting his attention. Yesterday, many had seemed of pressing urgency; today few seemed to demand his personal attention. He dictated a dozen or so letters into a tape-recorder, then sent the tape to an office near by for transcribing; it was a long time since he had employed a full-time secretary.

Next he glanced through his diary. There were several private sales, one of them in France, which he had planned to attend, as well as some important days at Sotheby's and Christies'. Larraby could do quite well as he himself, Mannering decided. There were now nine members of the sales staff, and two warehousemen at Quinns, all of whom knew their jobs thoroughly.

He sat back, chuckling.

"Raymond Li Chen couldn't have selected a better time!"

A few moments later he asked himself the question which had teased both him and Lorna: could there be any ulterior motive behind the invitation? On the spur of the moment he telephoned Christiansen, one of London's most famous dealers,

18

on the pretext of inquiring about a pair of fifteenth-century Toledo swords, and when he was about to ring off, he asked:

"Shall I see you in Hong Kong?"

Christiansen paused, it seemed for a long time. That did not really matter, and yet in a way it mattered a great deal.

"Oh, I've just realised what you mean," the other dealer said at last. "Li Chen's party. No, John, I don't think I can spare the time."

So the invitation had been general, and not particular to him; undoubtedly Lorna would be glad to hear that. Mannering pushed the vague premonitions away from him, trying to laugh them off. He had been involved so often in investigations and inquiries for missing jewels and valuables that he had become suspicious almost by second nature.

What clothes, if any, did he need to buy? He had sufficient tropical suits and lounge clothes, sufficient cabana sets, nearly everything. A pair or two of shoes and a shirt or two, and he would be properly set up. He would need travellers' cheques and perhaps letters of credit, in case he came across something he thought worth buying at one of the ports of call.

There wouldn't be time, except possibly in Bombay; in any case this was a holiday. His oldest friend in Bombay, old Phirozha, had died two years ago.

"No business at the ports of call," he decided firmly.

As he began to make a list of people whom he would normally see in the next few weeks, and whom he ought to talk to before he left, the telephone bell rang.

"Mannering of Quinns," he answered.

"Hold on, please," a girl said in the preoccupied manner of telephone operators the world over. "Mr. Bristow wants you."

The only Bristow whom Mannering knew was Superintendent William Bristow of New Scotland Yard.

*   *   *

It was unlikely that Bristow was calling to pass the time of day, or for any social reason. This would be official business.

19

Well, what about it? Mannering asked himself irritably. Bristow often called on some trifling inquiry. True, he hadn't done so for several weeks, but there had been long gaps between inquiries before. Why was he so sensitive this morning? And why was Bristow so long?

"You're through," the girl said at last.

"John?" Bristow's voice was as unmistakable as the sound of Bow Bells, not Cockney but unmistakably a Londoner's. "How busy are you?"

That was characteristic of the detective: to say a lot in a single brief sentence—and it would be characteristic of him to be acutely disappointed if Mannering were to say he was very busy indeed.

"Why?" Mannering asked guardedly, and added disarmingly: "How are you?"

"I'm all right." Bristow almost brushed the inquiry aside. "I'd like to talk to you about a job that's been dumped into my lap and which I don't think I can handle as well as you can."

"Never let it be said," retorted Mannering, and Bristow almost snapped a retort: "This is serious. Are you free for lunch?"

Strictly speaking, Mannering was free. He had intended to go and browse over the travel section of Hatchard's, not far away, and buy whatever books he thought would most attract Lorna, and he had planned to pick up some travel brochures on the way. Still, if he took Larraby's words at their face value, it didn't greatly matter whether he was in that afternoon or not.

"I could be," he said, still cautiously.

"Thanks. Will you meet me at Stanwell's at five to one?"

"Your treat?" inquired Mannering, almost unbelievingly.

"Yes," answered Bristow, quite brusquely. "I'll see you there."

He rang off, and Mannering did not fully realise for some minutes that he had allowed the Yard man to go without asking what he wanted to talk about.

"This isn't my morning," he said *sotto voce*. "It's certainly time I took a holiday."

He found himself chuckling again, and remained in the best of humours before leaving the shop at twenty minutes to one.

It was a bright crisp day. There was colour in the cheeks and a glow in the eyes of most Londoners in Bond Street and the narrow Mayfair streets which took him to Stanwell's. The restaurant was over one of London's oldest and quaintest of public houses, *My Lord of Mellon's*, and next to it, on a corner of a square as old if less renowned than Shepherd Market, was another antique and fine art shop—Ho's.

Ho's had once been owned by a Chinaman from Peking, but for many years it had been owned by two London Chinese who knew a great deal about oriental art. Their trade was more general than Mannering's, and there was a great deal of bric-à-brac in the windows which would never get house-room at Quinns; yet the window was attractively dressed, and possessed an unmistakable oriental dignity.

Mannering almost missed a step as he turned into the narrow entrance which led up even narrower stairs to Stanwell's, for suddenly he wondered why Bristow had chosen to meet him at this particular spot.

He tried to convince himself that this was simply coincidence, but he did not wholly suceed. It was nearly five to one when he entered the restaurant—and immediately Bristow stood up from a stool at the bar. Bristow was alone, a bigger man than he appeared to be because of his well-cut, snug-fitting pale-grey suit. It struck Mannering forcibly that Bristow didn't look a day older than he had twenty years ago. Even then his hair had been grey and close-trimmed; even then his clipped moustache had been stained yellow by nicotine, as it was now. He moved forward, hand outstretched, smiling, as if he was anxious to create a good impression.

"Hallo, John! Good of you to come."

"For such an occasion, what could keep me away?" asked Mannering. They shook hands, and stood facing each other, Mannering two inches taller, broader, and as dark-haired as

21

Bristow was grey. Bristow had good features which were somehow put together in a way which failed to make him handsome.

"What will you have?"

"Some beer at the table will suit me," Mannering said. "But don't let me stop you."

"Nothing would," Bristow answered him drily. They went to a corner table, so placed that they could not easily be overheard, and after a few courtesies, studied the menu.

"I think I'll have steak and kidney pudding," Mannering decided. "I probably won't have much chance of ye olde English fare for a few weeks, so I'll tuck in while the going's good."

As he had expected, and in fact intended, Bristow asked sharply:

"Are you going away?"

"Yes, Bill."

"Where?" inquired Bristow. He gave the impression that he would soon be very disappointed. Mannering feigned a deep interest in the comparative merits of cabbage and spinach, sauté and boiled potatoes, made his choice, looked smilingly into Bristow's eyes, and answered:

"A long way out of your reach, Bill. Lorna and I are going to Hong Kong."

"Hong Kong!" exclaimed Bristow. Instead of looking horrified he looked delighted, and so shattered the effect of Mannering's surprise. "That couldn't be better!" While Mannering was still recovering from the shock, the glow faded from the policeman's eyes and an intense stare replaced it. Quite suddenly, Bristow became a policeman on the hunt. "But it's too much for coincidence. You've been forewarned." He leaned forward, his manner was almost accusing. "Out with it, John. How much do you know?"

22

3

CAUSE FOR ALARM

THE hush over the table seemed to affect the small room; it was as if everyone near by was listening, even the barman who stood polishing a glass which reflected the array of vivid colours behind him. Mannering knew that Bristow was quite serious, and also knew that his reaction to the question affected him so that any answer would probably lack conviction.

"Nothing at all, Bill."

"There's no need to lie about it." The edge to Bristow's voice told of bad temper held in check; Bristow was never out of temper without good cause.

Mannering made himself smile, yet had an uneasy feeling that the smile looked forced; he still hadn't recovered from the shock of the question.

"Absolutely nothing, Bill, although if Lorna were sitting here she would probably be as sceptical as you are. I had an invitation to go to a special exhibition in Hong Kong—the centenary exhibition of one of the most reputable dealers there. Christiansen also had an invitation, I've no doubt all the major dealers have, and many of them will accept, you can be sure. It can be an expense charge against tax, which is quite an inducement." He stopped, expecting Bristow to make some comment, but the Yard man sat silently watching him, as if warily. Mannering began to feel annoyed. "Believe it or not, it's true."

Bristow picked up a half-smoked cigarette, and lit another from it.

"Yes, I can see it is. Sorry. It doesn't make sense, and it can't simply be coincidence. Or can it?" He stubbed out the old cigarette as he drew deeply on the other. "I've known some coincidences that no intelligent man would believe. Whose centenary is it?"

"Raymond Li Chen's," Mannering answered. "Of Li Chen Brothers."

23

"I've heard of the firm," Bristow conceded, "but not in this connection." He drew back as a waiter brought green pea soup for him, and *pâté maison* for Mannering. "Have you found more stuff coming from the Far East than usual?"

"If you'll tell me what you mean by stuff, I——"

"Oh, don't be so pernickety. You know perfectly well what I mean."

Mannering was so surprised by this outburst that he almost gaped. A waiter bringing the beer spilled a little, which splashed on to Bristow's soup spoon. Mannering half expected Bristow to snap at the man as he apologised and dabbed with his snow-white napkin.

"Leave it alone," Bristow said gruffly, and the man moved off. Bristow deliberately avoided Mannering's eye, and scooped up soup. He was so touchy that obviously he was labouring under a great strain, and Mannering selected the soft answer:

"I haven't noticed much more in the way of jewellery or precious stones, but there are a lot of new and old ivory carvings, and some jade as well as rose quartz on the market. Some of it's very valuable, but it's never been my special interest. What's worrying you about it?"

"A lot of it is being stolen from China, smuggled into Hong Kong, and then into England." Bristow finished his soup, and forced a smile, not yet himself but obviously trying to be. "Much is reproduction, and liable to heavy duty. I've been handling it for months. Two or three small collections turned up in London shops and the shopkeepers swear they didn't know it was smuggled in. We've been working with the Hong Kong police. I thought it was just another routine investigation. This morning I spent an hour with the Commissioner and the Assistant Commissioner, who think I've neglected the job. It's reached top level. So many valuables are being brought out of Peking, Canton, Hankow, and Shanghai that the Chinese top brass made a song and dance about it. Everyone's so bloody sensitive about hurting the Commies' feelings you'd think I'd committed a major crime." Bristow's grin was fierce but much

24

more natural. "Now you know why I'm in such a foul mood."

"Know and understand," said Mannering commiseratingly. "If it's worth top level action it must be very big."

"They talk in millions of pounds worth stolen from China," Bristow reported.

"A million pounds can buy a lot of Canadian wheat for Peking,' Mannering murmured. "I can see why they're so touchy, too. Have you had any luck at all?"

"Not to say luck. Two of the small collections were sold from next door—Ho's. They say they bought them from American dealers; they've the invoices, receipts, customs forms, everything to make it look legal. The third collection was up for auction at Sotheby's, among the estate of a man who died last autumn. No one knows where he got it from, but he had a good reputation, and there's no erason to doubt that he came by it honestly. He was a customer of Ho's."

"How much was each collection worth?"

"The largest about ten thousand pounds, the others around three thousand each. I know, I know; not much to set against a million or so."

A waiter pushed along the trolley, on which stood a steaming steak and kidney pudding, and vegetables being kept hot over a spirit lamp. Bristow ate as if he were famished, and Mannering sank himself into the succulence of the meal. Thoughts drifted through his mind, inconclusively, and only now and again did he feel any cause at all for alarm—or for the fear that Li Chen had really invited him because of these problems.

"Any reason to think that Ho's would touch stolen or smuggled goods and sell them in their shop?" demanded Bristow suddenly.

"None at all," answered Mannering promptly. "Exactly what do you want me to do, Bill?"

Bristow appeared to reflect, although there was no doubt that he had come here knowing exactly what he wanted. Would he change his mind or his approach because of Mannering's projected trip?

"I want you to find out if there is any unusual activity in this particular market," said Bristow at last. "Inquire among your friends in the trade and make a comprehensive report—particularly if anyone is trying to dispose of an unusually big collection. What I hoped..." he broke off, as if resignedly. "Forget it."

"What did you hope?"

"It's not practical now."

"You can still tell me what it is."

"You won't have time," gloomed Bristow. "I hoped you could find out something which would enable me to convince the top brass that I haven't been asleep. I—er——" Bristow broke off, and Mannering saw the unbelievable; the Yard man was almost blushing. "I told them that I'd consulted you earlier, but hadn't heard from you."

Mannering simply sat and grinned.

"That's right, be smug," growled Bristow. "The truth is I neglected the job. We've plenty of crime in London without spending much time on routine affairs from overseas."

"Only this wasn't routine," said Mannering. "Like to add one more white lie to the other?"

"What?" asked Bristow, almost suspiciously.

"Tell your chaps that I've come to the conclusion that this can only be handled in Hong Kong, and that your highly respected consultant is going to see what he can find out there. That ought to mollify everyone."

Bristow chuckled, as if for the first time he felt free from strain.

"Good idea," he approved. "And it's true, isn't it?"

"What's true?"

"That when you're in Hong Kong you will see what you can find out for me. How long will you be there?"

"About two weeks."

"Well then, you'll have plenty of time. Lorna will be so busy shopping and having exotic dresses made that you'll find time hanging on your hands."

There was nothing Mannering could do but say "yes", and

there was no point in allowing Bristow to see his misgivings. But for the talk with Lorna, and the intrusion of those fears from the past, he would probably not have thought twice about it. He was quite sure that Lorna would be highly sensitive to any suggestion that he should work in Hong Kong, even if it really meant just "keeping his eyes open".

When he left Bristow at a corner near Stanwell's and Ho's, Mannering walked slowly towards Piccadilly. He was very thoughtful as he went into Hatchards and browsed among the books. He was back at Quinns a little after three-thirty, and when he reached the narrow-fronted window he pulled up with a start.

Placed on black velvet was a beautiful and most elegant creation in duck-egg blue; a Ming dynasty vase. He had forgotten that it was in the vaults. Obviously Larraby, who had dressed the window after he had left for lunch, had been influenced by the talk of China and Hong Kong.

Studying the vase Mannering found himself smiling. Then he realised that instead of being in any way depressed by Bristow he was if anything excited. Now he had much more than an exhibition and holiday to look forward to. The only disquieting factor was Lorna's reaction.

*   *   *

"I suppose it was inevitable," Lorna said resignedly. "I didn't really believe that you would be able to take a long holiday without something interfering. You'll be happier, really, won't you?"

"Happier?" echoed Mannering, as if astonished.

Lorna laughed; and it was good to know that she was not really worried. She was still eager and excited, surrounded by brochures they had collected, and the books which Mannering had bought. "The main thing is to get you away from London for a few weeks." More thoughtfully, she went on: "I wonder if your friend Raymond Li Chen knows anything about this. He couldn't have stolen this missing stuff for display at his exhibition, could he?"

27

"Stuff!" echoed Mannering. "You're as bad as Bristow."

*　　　*　　　*

The next five days passed with bewildering swiftness. There were people to see, plans to make, passports to check—there seemed no time to do anything properly, certainly no time to brood or even ponder over thefts from Communist China. At odd moments Mannering wondered whether Bristow had found anything out, but he made no attempt to find out.

Tuesday dawned clear and bright and very cold. The *Orienta* was to sail from King Albert Docks at twelve-thirty, and Lorna was up at six for a final flurry of packing, with the help of two daily maids. Mannering, intending not to go to the office, called to check with Larraby, who said:

"Do you think you could possibly call in for a few minutes, sir?"

"Is it really necessary?"

"I think you would think so," Larraby said guardedly.

Lorna was so involved that she hardly seemed to hear Mannering, although she said:

"You'll be back in good time, won't you?"

"By eleven at the latest."

"They won't keep the ship waiting for us, you know."

Mannering went off in a hired car with a chauffeur, and reached the back of the shop at a quarter to ten. It was locked as always. He unlocked it and stepped inside the dark store-room. The door leading to the shop itself was ajar, and as he pushed this open he saw Larraby standing with something in his hands—and with a grave expression on his face. For the first time Mannering realised that the summons had really been a harbinger of trouble.

"What is it, Josh?" he asked—and immediately saw what Larraby held.

It was a piece of the pale-blue Ming vase—a single piece, perhaps a quarter of the whole vase.

Mannering was appalled.

It was not simply the value of the vase, for however this had

28

come about, insurance would cover it. It was the sudden realisation that so beautiful a thing, unique as well as centuries old, should be broken. At moments like these he knew how much he cared for the intrinsic value of the precious things he dealt in.

Larraby looked so heartbroken that it seemed to Mannering that he must have dropped it himself.

"I feel terrible," Larraby said. "Terrible."

"I'm sure you do. But you haven't had a serious accident all the years you've been with me, so——"

"This was no accident," Larraby said. "This was smashed deliberately."

*　　　*　　　*

Larraby relived the moments as he stood holding the piece of precious pottery.

He had taken the vase out of the window, the previous night, and put it in the strong-room, as he always did. Today was to be the last day for its display.

He had carried it cradled in his arms as if it were a living child, towards the window. He saw a man standing at the empty window, which was unusual, as he pulled aside the black velvet. Two junior assistants stood near, and one of them would keep the vase in sight all day—there would be no moment when it was not under surveillance. There was a special safety device at the window, as well as a microphone outside in the street which picked up even whispered words. More than one thief had been forestalled by that precaution.

Larraby saw that the man at the window was an Oriental, and assumed without really thinking that he was Chinese. There still seemed no cause for alarm or anxiety. Larraby placed the vase in position, and stood back to admire it yet again. In the subdued light, the lustrous surface seemed to glow.

The shop door opened. One of the assistants moved forward.

"Good morning, sir. What——"

Larraby heard the gasp of alarm, swung round, saw the man fling something, some dark object, at the vase. Larraby thrust his arm up and deflected the missile, which caught the neck of the precious thing.

*   *   *

"The vase crashed against the window," Larraby told Mannering unhappily. "The man ran out and escaped, I'm afraid. We were all so terribly shocked, but even when I had recovered I hesitated to send for the police."

"Why?" Mannering asked. He realised for the first time that no police were here, that this crime had not yet been reported.

Larraby answered quietly: "If I sent for them they would want to see you, sir. Word would reach the Press, and you would be besieged on board ship. I know how much you and Mrs. Mannering have been looking forward to this voyage, and I hate to think of spoiling it in any way. But you had to know." He moistened his lips. "What shall we do, Mr. Mannering? Report it as an accident? No one but the staff saw what happened, and they will be discreet, I'm sure."

Mannering said quietly: "No, Josh. Tell the police this afternoon. Talk to Bristow and tell him why you left it so late." His mind was working very quickly, a dozen thoughts flashed through it. "There's little chance of tracing the man who did it—what kind of description did you get?"

"Except that he was oriental, I noticed very little," Larraby answered. "He was small, and I think quite young. What baffles me is why anyone should commit such vandalism. The vase was so very, very beautiful." There was a catch in his voice. "You agree that I was right to let you know, don't you?"

"Absolutely right," agreed Mannering. "Keep me informed of anything that happens as a result of this—by radio-telephone or radio-telegram if necessary. We won't ease the situation by pretending that it didn't happen."

"It could hardly be a less auspicious start to your voyage,

sir," Larraby said, and he added miserably: "There is nothing I would have liked to avoid more."

He stopped, looking so unhappy that Mannering forced his own depression away. He heard footsteps in the street, the sound caught by the microphone coming clearly into the shop. He looked towards the window as two men passed it, and stopped at the door. Both were small, both were oriental, and even at this distance he felt sure that they were Chinese.

4

THE TWO CHINAMEN

MANNERING heard Larraby catch his breath at the sight of the two men. He saw Winchester, a youthful-looking assistant who had boxed for Cambridge, move towards the door as if aggressively. The two newcomers were immaculately dressed in brown suits and fawn-coloured overcoats, and each wore a wide-brimmed trilby which matched his suit. They moved together with such precision that they seemed to be operated by clockwork.

"Recognise either of them?" Mannering asked Larraby in a whisper.

"These are much older men," Larraby answered.

They had stopped in front of Winchester, whose broad shoulders hid them from sight. Courteously, he asked:

"Can I help you, gentlemen?"

"We wish to see Mr. John Mannering, please."

"I'm sorry but Mr. Mannering is not available today." Winchester began the routine excuse, but stopped abruptly, for the Chinamen came on. He swayed to one side to baulk them, and as he did so the Chinaman on the left swerved in the other direction, and then swayed past him. It was a remarkable feat of balance and body swerve, and foxed Winchester completely.

31

He nearly fell, saved himself, and swung round. Both callers were now approaching Mannering along the strip of wine-red carpet which ran the length of the shop, and both were staring fixedly at Mannering. It was impossible to be sure they were smiling, but their teeth were bared.

"Mr. Mannering——" Larraby began, in alarm.

With precision which matched that of the two Chinamen, two more of Quinns' assistants moved in their path, and again both men were cut off from sight. Mannering watched, so fascinated that he almost forgot the tragedy of the Ming vase.

Surely the body-swerving visitor could not evade these two.

Mannering actually saw what happened, but simply could not tell how it was done. One of his young men said just as politely as Winchester:

"I'm sorry, sir, but Mr. Mannering is not——" and then he stopped and moved swiftly to one side. The second assistant went in the other direction. There was a mix-up which was almost a mêlée, before the two Chinamen marched, unimpeded, towards Mannering. Two young men began to pick themselves up from the floor, slowly.

"Mr. Mannering!" breathed Larraby.

"Mr. Mannering," said the Chinaman on the left, "please will you give me a little time?" He smiled and inclined his head as he spoke, and the tone of his voice suggested a kind of humility. The other man stared at Mannering without speaking, but with unmistakable pleading in his brown eyes.

"Would you like to come into my office?" said Mannering. "We can talk until the police arrive."

He watched both men intently, and noticed the two things. The speaker was badly shaken by the word "police", and the other, older man's expression did not change: either he was deaf or he did not understand English.

"Police?" echoed the first man. "I do not understand."

"You forced your way past my assistants, using considerable violence. That is called assault in this country."

"Assault," echoed the first man as if he did not really know

32

the meaning of the word. "I must talk to you, Mr. Mannering, it is extremely urgent."

"They both told you that I wasn't available," Mannering pointed out. "I'm going on a long voyage, and my ship is due to sail this morning. So if you will excuse me——"

He broke off, in turn. The speaker hardly seemed to move, but suddenly his right hand clutched Mannering's wrist. Mannering sensed the power of the grip, feared what would happen if he tried to wrench himself free. Behind the two Chinamen, one of whom was staring at him with such mute appeal, all three of the humiliated assistants were drawing closer, but the visitors seemed oblivious of any possibility of danger.

"You must listen to me," the speaker insisted. "Do you understand? *Listen to me.*"

Winchester was very close behind him, and mouthed the words: "Shall I deal with him?" The Chinaman must have been aware of this, but took no notice.

"If I were you I'd watch the doors—back and front," advised Mannering. "These two might not be alone." He made no attempt to free himself, but went on: "Telephone the police right away, Josh."

Larraby moved towards a telephone on a table at the back of the shop. Mannering felt pressure tightening on his wrist, and wondered fleetingly whether these men were in fact Japanese.

The telephone went *ting!* as Larraby picked up the receiver.

Pressure grew into pain on Mannering's wrist. There was no spoken threat, yet the threat was unmistakable: "send for the police at your peril". The strangest part of all was the intensity of the silent man's gaze, and of the appeal in his soft eyes.

"If you break my wrist nothing can save you from prison." Mannering did not raise his voice, and there was no tremor in it, but in fact he felt afraid. The man could undoubtedly break his wrist, as he or someone like him had smashed the Ming vase. If he did, that would spoil every minute of the voyage, distress Lorna, perhaps even handicap his movements for a long, long time.

33

Larraby was saying urgently into the telephone: "Super-intendent Bristow, please." He was looking at Mannering as if afraid that at any moment his bone would snap; he seemed to be gritting his teeth. The Chinaman, gripping Mannering's wrist, exerted such pressure that pain streaked up Mannering's arm to the elbow.

"Let me go," Mannering ordered, still quite calmly.

"Mr. Bristow, hold on a moment, please, Mr. Mannering would like a word with you."

The pause which followed seemed to last for a very long time. No one moved. The men at the doors looked as if they were carved out of stone. Larraby put the receiver down on a padded stool, and went on in a quivering voice: "For God's sake let him go."

The Chinaman released Mannering, and allowed his arm to drop to his side. It felt numbed and limp, as if all strength had been drained from it, but he turned and picked up the telephone with his uninjured right hand. He watched the two Chinamen as he said:

"Sorry to keep you, Bill. I thought you ought to know that someone seems very determined to keep me here in England. They'll fail, but they're trying very hard."

"Have you any idea who they are?" asked Bristow; he sounded as if he could hardly wait to find out.

"Only that they are Chinese," said Mannering carefully. "I'll let you have a full description as soon as I can. Meanwhile, if Josh Larraby needs any help, see that he gets it at once, won't you?"

He rang off without waiting for Bristow to speak again, turned towards the office door, and said:

"I'll spare you five minutes, not one minute more." As he stood aside for the Chinamen to enter, he went on to Larraby: "There'll be an urgent errand after this, Josh."

"I quite understand, sir. Are you sure you'll be all right?"

"Leave the door open. I'll shout if I need help!"

When Mannering moved behind his desk and sat down, pins and needles were shooting up his left arm. He had to clench

34

and unclench his hand to try and keep the pain at bay, but at least it grew no worse.

The Chinaman who had not yet uttered a word was smiling, as if delighted; it now seemed obvious that he was very old—older perhaps by twenty years than the man who had so nearly broken Mannering's arm. The younger man's teeth were hidden now and his lips were taut; he looked as if he was struggling to restrain himself.

"Half a minute's gone already," Mannering said coldly. "What do you want?"

"We want your help."

"You've a peculiar way of showing it. What kind of help?"

"Your professional help," the Chinaman went on. "We wish you, please, to examine and value for us a great hoard of precious stones and beautiful carvings, many jewels and pieces of ivory, jade and precious metals, all magnificent in every way. Nothing so magnificent has ever before been together in one place, but they are here, in London. We wish you to value them for us," he repeated, "because we have been told that you are a great expert, and also an honest man. It is very urgent—very, very urgent. Please. Will you?"

All the time he had been talking, his voice had been changing, until now it was pitched very high, as if he wanted to command yet knew that his only hope was to plead. His companion did not once look away from Mannering; it was almost possible to believe that tears caused the sheen in his eyes.

"Please, please, please," he seemed to be pleading.

Mannering asked: "Where is this remarkable collection?" He only just managed to keep a sneer out of his voice.

"It is here, in London."

"I might just have time to look——"

"You must spend much, much time with them," the younger Chinaman declared imperiously. "It will take days, perhaps several weeks. And you are the only man who can be relied on."

"Please, *please*," pleaded the luminous old eyes.

35

"Exactly where do you keep them?" Mannering asked, as if he were wavering.

"You will come?"

"How far away is it?"

"Not very far," the Chinaman said. "They are stored in a very safe place indeed. Mr. Mannering"—he seemed to find it harder to keep his temper, and the words were painfully shrill —"you may sell this collection for us. It will mean a big fortune for you. Nothing else is important."

"Where is it?" Mannering kept on trying.

"Not far from here. Come with us and we will show you. Please, Mr. Mannering. Even if you cannot spend much time, come and see. Come and feast your eyes on the glories of China's past, on jewels which belonged to the emperors and the war-lords, jewels which until these days did not once leave our native land. When you see them for yourself, nothing will make you go away and leave them."

He spoke as if he believed that all to be true. Mannering knew well that he might be speaking even more truly than he realised. In a strange, almost unnatural way, Mannering felt the stirring of excitement. The lure of stones and rare and precious things was strong, almost irresistible. Talk of jewels could affect him deeply, even before he set eyes on them. Rare jewels which he actually saw and handled had an effect on him almost like a drug. This man seemed to know that talking about such things might weaken his resolve. The older man played a silent part, too. His eyes seemed to have a mesmeric effect.

Oh, it was nonsense! But there they were fixed unwaveringly on him, willing him to say "yes". Already more than five minutes had passed, so they had achieved a partial victory.

They had done more; they had half convinced him that the stolen hoard Bristow had talked about was here in London. He owed it to Bristow, to the police, to try and find out if that were true. Once glance would be all he needed; yet one glance might be enough to make him want to stay and gloat over the jewels, examining each one with a connoisseur's devotion.

36

It *was* like a drug; and it was ludicrous.

"Mr. Mannering." Larraby's voice pierced the quiet. "It is getting very late."

"Yes, I know."

"You're due to leave for the docks in less than an hour, and it will take half an hour to get home."

"Yes, yes," Mannering said almost impatiently.

He could go and make sure whether this collection was in London, and if it were he could tell Bristow. At a pinch Lorna could go ahead to the ship and he could join her on board; there was no need to consider flying to Hong Kong.

There was another sound, farther away; the opening of the shop door. Almost at once Larraby exclaimed: "Mr. Bristow!"

"Bristow!" echoed Mannering.

"Who is that?" the Chinaman demanded sharply. "The police?" He half turned, staring through the partly open doorway.

An assistant said: "Good—good morning, Superintendent."

"Good morning." That was unmistakably Bristow. "Where is Mannering? Is he still here?"

*   *   *

It was useless to ask himself what had brought Bristow here so quickly, and it did not really matter. Sanity seemed to drop upon Mannering like a cloak. He saw the younger of the two men move, but before he could go far he gripped him above his right elbow, and held him fast in a lock he could not break. The man who had not uttered a word shuffled back, mouth agape, almond-shaped eyes rounded as if in horror—and as if he could not even begin to understand what had happened. All this time Bristow came marching along the middle of the shop, footsteps muffled but not silenced by the thick pile of the carpet.

"Mr. Mannering," said the man in Mannering's grasp. "If you keep me here you will regret it all your life."

As he spoke, Bristow appeared; and in that moment

37

Mannering had a strange feeling, almost a conviction, that what he said was not so much a threat as a simple statement of fact.

Larraby said something which Mannering did not catch.

"Hallo," Bristow said. "What's this, John?"

There was still time to release the Chinaman and pretend that there was nothing amiss; Bristow might not believe him, but could not do much about it. One call to the other assistants, one moment of relaxation, and the man could be on his way.

Why was the temptation so great that it was almost irresistible?

"Mr. Mannering, the *time*," urged Larraby.

Bristow now maintained a puzzled silence, as if he also was aware of a tension he did not wish to break.

Suddenly Mannering let his captive go, and said in a dry, hoarse voice:

"This man wants me to take a look at the greatest collection of jewels and *objets d'art* ever to leave China. He didn't say they were honestly come by, you'll have to make sure of that. I've a ship to catch."

Bristow said: "Well, well!"

The man whom Mannering had held turned on him, his face distorted in an expression which seemed to mingle hatred with fury, and fury with malevolence. Mannering could not make himself look anywhere but into those burning eyes.

The man spat into his face, swung round, and leapt forward, as if believing he could pass all the men in the shop and get away. That was the moment when the other Chinaman uttered his first sound, a hoarse, almost guttural cry.

As he did so, he collapsed against Mannering; and at the same time the other man sent Bristow and Larraby flying, and disappeared from the office into the shop.

5
SIGHT TO SEE

MANNERING thrust the old man away from him, and pushed past a staggering Bristow into the shop. Then he stood still, staring at an incredible sight. The width of carpet leading to the front door seemed to be littered with young men in dark clothes, sprawling, gasping, at least one of them groaning. How that miniature Chinaman had caused such havoc it was impossible to guess. Now he was within two yards of the door, which was closed. Two women in the street were looking at model hats, and had their backs to Quinns; no one else was in sight out there; if the Chinaman reached the street he would probably escape.

There was one adversary to be reckoned with; young Winchester.

He was in front of the elusive little Chinaman, with his back to the door. Half crouching, he gave the impression that he knew that the other would fool him. He was weaving from side to side. Mannering took in all of that in a split second, then saw the Chinaman feint, and Winchester go in the wrong direction. Mannering almost groaned.

Then Winchester swayed to the other side; he had fooled the Chinaman! At the same moment, Winchester flung himself forward, and crashed into his adversary. Both fell, the Chinaman backwards, Winchester on top of him like a ton weight. Mannering heard Bristow catch his breath, and on that instant understood why. The Chinaman was falling slantwise, and his hat fell off when he was only inches from the corner of an Elizabethan court cupboard on which a dozen pieces of Georgian silver shone and glimmered.

There was a sickening crunch of sound. The Chinaman's body did a funny little shivering twist before it crashed to the carpet, and flopped inert. Winchester turned his shoulder to the floor, and took his weight on it. Before he even began to

39

get up, Mannering and Bristow were rushing towards the Chinaman. At least no blood showed. Bristow reached the man first, and knelt over him, straightening his body and then feeling gingerly for the wound in his head. The others gathered round, one man helping Winchester to his feet. Mannering spared a glance and a "Nice work, Guy," as Bristow said:

"Doesn't seem to be broken."

"It's a nice smooth corner," Mannering remarked, running his hand over the oak darkened by centuries of polishing. "Think you need a doctor for him?"

"Shall I telephone for one?" asked Larraby.

Bristow was prodding gently but firmly, and at the same time feeling the Chinaman's pulse.

"I don't think it's necessary, but it might be wise. It might be wise to make sure he can't fox us, too." He took a pair of slender handcuffs out of his fob pocket, where they did not spoil the fit of his trousers, clipped one round the Chinaman's tiny, bony wrist, and the other round the cross-piece of a stout William and Mary slung chair. "That'll hold him." He straightened up. "What time are you due to sail, John?"

"Half past twelve," Mannering replied.

"Did Larraby hear everything this man said?"

Before Mannering could answer Larraby declared emphatically: "Every word, sir."

"Then you'd better get off," Bristow said to Mannering. "If there's any need, I can telephone you on the ship."

"Yes," said Mannering. "Yes, you can. Thank you, Bill."

The truth was, of course, that he did not want to go. The unconscious man might have told the truth, and that fabulous collection might be here in London; he yearned to see it. It was exasperating and even ludicrous, but above everything at that moment he wanted to stay and see this thing through.

Obviously Larraby sensed his mood.

"Mrs. Mannering will be very anxious, sir."

"Yes, won't she?" Mannering forced himself to look away from the man on the floor. He grinned suddenly, clapped Bristow on the shoulder, swung round to Larraby and gripped his hand. "Josh, look after everything. Tell the Superintendent the sad story of the Ming vase, and don't keep anything back." He shook hands with Winchester, who looked rather like an overgrown schoolboy, slightly red in the face, at least twice the size of the man he had felled. "If you hadn't had your wits about you, we'd have lost him, Guy. Thanks." He raised his right arm in a comprehensive wave to everyone else in the shop. "Goodbye, all. See you in the Spring!" He swung round and strode into the office for his briefcase, saw the other Chinaman sitting in a carved Jacobean chair, pale as death but breathing. "He looks almost like Confucius," he confided to Larraby, who was just behind him, then went striding out the back way to the waiting car, without glancing behind him. It was utterly ridiculous—of course he wanted to go! In fact he could hardly wait to get aboard that ship. Anyhow the little Chinaman had certainly been lying.

Had he?

What reason could he have for such lies except the improbable one of trying to keep Mannering in London?

"I must forget it," Mannering told himself as he sat back in the car. "I've got to make Lorna believe that everything's as right as can be."

*　　　*　　　*

The suitcases, seven of them, were already at the front porch, brought down one by one in the tiny lift. Two hanging bags, containing Lorna's dresses, were draped over the banister rail. Mannering stepped out of the lift into the small hall of their flat, and heard Lorna saying: "I'll send you a card from time to time, and give you plenty of notice when we're coming back. If you need to get in touch with us, Larraby at the shop will know where to find us." Lorna glanced up, saw Mannering, and smiled a bright welcome. "Hallo, darling! I'm absolutely ready."

"Give me two minutes," said Mannering.

He was ready in three minutes, level. They paused to take a last glance round at the apartment they had not left for so long

41

a period for many years, two dailies—one young, one middle-aged—watching them.

Mannering put his arm round Lorna's waist, and squeezed.

"We're off!" he cried. "Next stop Hong Kong!" He strode to the lift, which was open, handed Lorna in, and stepped in beside her. "If you weren't so beautifully made up, I'd spoil your lipstick."

Her eyes were glowing.

"You're as excited as I am," she said. "I was afraid you wouldn't be."

That was exactly what he wanted her to feel.

When they reached the street level, all the baggage was loaded in a second hired car. Mannering and Lorna got into the first. The two dailies, the milkman, a neighbour, and a postman gathered, as it were, to see them off. They swung out of the street on to the Embankment, towards the smiling river. Ten miles along its winding, silvered length was the Port of London, and in the King Albert Dock a great ship was waiting to carry them across the seas.

A man turned the corner, and stared at them. He was small and impeccably dressed, and looked as if he could be the brother of the Chinaman who had been unconscious in the shop.

Lorna did not see him. Mannering made no comment as he sat back. He tried to convince himself that it was coincidence, there were many thousands of Chinese in London and as many other Orientals who weren't very different in appearance. Yet now and again he glanced out of the back window, if he felt sure Lorna would not notice, because he half suspected that the Chinaman might be following them.

There was no sight of anyone on their heels, and he did not see the man again. By the time they reached the East End, Mannering had stopped looking, but as they drove along the narrow streets and passed the tiny terraced houses, he saw not one but dozens of Chinese, men, women, and children, all as ordinary as could be, and certainly taking no notice of him.

They turned into the docks. A policeman at the main gate—No. 7—saluted them, but that was probably an ordinary courtesy. The elderly driver of the car knew the way, and soon they saw the solitary beige-coloured funnel of the *Orienta* rising high above the wharves and warehouses. As they drew near, Mannering saw that the booms had been shipped, showing that loading was finished. A small man with a shiny, rosy face checked their tickets, and immigration was a formality.

"Your baggage will go direct to your cabin," the shiny-faced man told them. "You're free to go aboard now."

There was a radiance in Lorna's eyes, and it was easy to see she had not really believed the voyage would actually take place. She preceded him up the gangway, and at the ship's hall a serge-clad steward asked:

"What cabin, sir? ... A31, this way, please." He led the way down one flight of stairs and past hundreds of people. Here and there among them were Chinamen and an occasional Chinese family. What was surprising about that in a ship going to Hong Kong and Singapore?

The steward turned into a passage-way and opened the door of A31. Quite suddenly, and for no reason other than nervous tension, Mannering pushed past Lorna into the room.

Lorna exclaimed: "John!"

The room was a mass of flowers, huge bouquets and sheaths and bunches, some in vases, some in bowls, some on the beds and some even on the floor. The scent of flowers was heavy on the air and their beauty was quite indescribable.

"I've never seen anything like it," Lorna said, after a long pause. She sounded husky. "Everyone who knows we're sailing must have sent some." She stood in the middle of the room, while Mannering watched her and scoffed at his own fears.

One thing was absolutely certain: he must do nothing to spoil the send-off for her. He would have to tell her what had happened later, days later, if possible.

"Your steward will be along for your ticket soon, sir," said the man who had escorted them here. "He'll get you anything you want." He went off, while Lorna gazed about her, then

43

saw a pile of telegrams on the dressing-table. The mirror behind them showed her almost full-length—mink coat and mink hat dark and richly brown, cheeks flushed—as she picked up the telegrams.

"One for you," she said, and began to open the others. Mannering stepped to the ports, one over a bed, one at the foot of a bed, and saw a few men standing about on the quayside, and some baggage being carried by dockers and porters. No one seemed to take any particular interest in this room. He half laughed at himself; how could anyone know which ports were theirs?

"One from the Plenders," Lorna was saying. "And one from Larraby . . . One from the curator at the Royal Academy, isn't that nice of him? . . . One from . . ."

Mannering heard her but did not catch the words after that, for he opened his own, and read:

"You'll be a fool if you go, no good can come of it."

That was all. There was no signature, nothing to indicate who had sent it. It had been handed in in central London only an hour and a half ago. He glanced at Lorna, who was chuckling.

"Listen to this: 'Now you've got him away keep him away.' Guess who that's from?"

"I give up," said Mannering promptly.

"Bill Bristow! Everyone seems determined to give us a wonderful send-off. Who is yours from?"

Before Mannering could answer, a steward appeared at the door.

"Mr. Mannering?"

"Yes."

"There's a telephone call for you, sir. And also some reporters would very much like to have a word with you. I told them I wasn't sure whether you were on board yet, not being sure you would want to be worried by them."

"If I know the Press, they'll find a way to worry us," said Mannering. "Aren't the phones through in the room?"

"Not for outside calls, sir."

44

"You stay here," Mannering said to Lorna. "I'll need some help when the newspaper-men arrive."

"You'll need a lot of help!" She had forgotten his telegram, and started to open another addressed to *Mr. and Mrs.* He followed the steward, a grey-haired, mellow and quiet-voiced man, as far as the hall on 'A' deck. Three newspaper-men and two photographers were spilling down the stairs.

"Mr. Mannering!"

"Just the man we want!"

"Can you spare us a few minutes, sir?"

"As soon as I've taken a telephone call," Mannering said. "My wife is in the cabin, and she's much more photogenic than I."

They moved *en masse* along the passage, one man calling: "A31, isn't it?"

The stairs were crowded, and a voice was sounding over the ship's broadcasting system:

"All visitors ashore, please. The *Orienta* is due to sail in fifteen minutes. All visitors ashore, please." There was a bustle and a flurry of goodbyes. Near the telephone booths a man stood grave-faced alongside a woman in tears. Mannering had to squeeze past them to get into the booth; he doubted whether either noticed him.

"This is John Mannering," he said to the operator.

"Oh yes, sir, I have a call for you. Just one moment, please."

The most likely person to call was Bristow; almost certainly Larraby wouldn't trouble him now, and he had tied up all the loose ends of routine at the shop. The moment became a minute, and he began to feel impatient. A smiling Chinese woman and a poker-faced Chinese man stood only a few yards away, talking to an Englishman who was big enough to be a policeman. Absurd thought, reflected Mannering; what was the matter with him today? Fact and fantasy were all mixed up in his mind.

Why the blazes didn't the caller——

A man spoke in a soft voice:

45

"Mr. Mannering?"

"What is it?" said Mannering, brusquely.

"Mr. Mannering," the man said again, "that Ming vase was of very great value. You know that."

Mannering caught his breath. Only the people in the shop and the vandal who had smashed the vase knew what had happened.

"You understand me, Mr. Mannering?" The hint of a lisp was more pronounced, *Mister* became almost *Mithter*.

"I know how much that vase was worth," Mannering said in a hard voice. "Between three and four thousand pounds. Did you break it?"

After a hesitant pause the caller said, as if with quiet pride: "Yes, I did so, Mr. Mannering. At your very beautiful and venerable shop you have many other beautiful works of art, I am sure. If you do not go to Hong Kong, all will be well, no more will be damaged. But if you go . . ."

The man broke off. Almost at once there was the click of the receiver being replaced.

Outside, the poker-faced Chinaman was still talking to the big Englishman, but glancing at Mannering from time to time. People passed to and fro. There was a blast on the ship's whistle, which sounded very loud. The operator said apologetically: "I'm afraid we've been disconnected, Mr. Mannering. We are about to sail."

"I know," Mannering said. "I've finished, thanks. When do the newspaper-men leave the ship?"

"They'll be leaving in a launch when we enter the river at Tilbury, I expect, sir."

"Thanks." Mannering stepped out of the booth, and brushed his hand across his forehead; it came away damp. His mind was seething with the inevitable questions. He had to get word to Bristow, and make sure that the Yard appreciated the seriousness of the threat.

A young steward approached.

"Mr. Mannering?"

"Yes," Mannering said bleakly.

46

"A Chinese gentleman who went ashore asked me to give you this, sir." He handed Mannering a sealed envelope, and went off. Mannering stood with the envelope in his hand, almost sure this would be another move in the attempt to make him turn back—but suddenly it occurred to him that whoever had sent the message knew that he was still on board. He ripped open the envelope, unfolded the heavy cream-laid paper inside, and read: *"You may leave the ship at Bombay. No later."*

6

SHIP AT SEA

MANNERING was tempted to screw the note up and toss it aside, but he did not. It was typewritten, and typewriters could be traced. He looked about the nearly empty hall, seeing a crowd jostling at the ship's rail only a few yards away. He and Lorna ought to be out there, seeing London for the last time for weeks. Well, they weren't on deck, and Lorna was being kept busy by the men of the Press. He went downstairs and along the passage which passed his cabin; at least four men and two women were inside, and all of them seemed to be talking and laughing together—Lorna's voice was easily distinguishable, high-pitched and gay.

Mannering turned round and hurried to the writing-room; only one oldish man was there, reading. Mannering sat and wrote a letter so quickly that the pen seemed to fly over the paper; it told Bristow of the threat to the stock at Quinns, and the "Bombay or else" note. He folded that note inside the envelope in which it had been sent, addressed another to Bristow at the Yard, a third to Larraby at Quinns. He put the first two into Larraby's envelope with a curt: *"Deliver this personally to Bristow."* He slipped the letter into his pocket, and went out. People were drifting away from the ship's rails, but there were still plenty on deck. The commotion in A31 was quite remarkable. Lorna talking about an exhibition at the Tate, goodness knows why. Mannering pushed his way towards her. No one wanted her to finish, and she was obviously on top form.

"... and even if it is by Picasso it isn't necessarily good, sometimes his virtuosity is simply for effect—tongue in cheek, probably." That was one of her favourite themes. She looked up, saw Mannering, called: "Hallo, John!" To the others she said laughingly: "Here's my husband. He's really the one you want to see."

Mannering laughed in turn.

"Don't put them on the spot. None of them knows whether they dare agree with you, in case they affront you."

Someone laughed ...

Ten minutes or so later, the last of the men was about to leave the cabin; the two women were still talking to Lorna. If they were not careful they would be late for the launch at Tilbury.

"See this gets to my man at Quinns, will you?" Mannering asked the reporter. "It's something I'd forgotten. If you could get it to him today I'd be most grateful."

"It's as good as there," the reporter promised. "Have a good trip, Mr. Mannering. Your wife says it's the first real holiday you've had in ten years."

The first real holiday ...

Mannering found himself chuckling, almost ruefully. The two reporters passed him, calling back to Lorna, and Mannering went farther into the cabin. Lorna, hat off, hair a little untidy, still flushed, looked almost like the blushing bride, and the cabin a bridal bower. She pushed her fingers lightly through her hair, glanced into the mirror, said: "At least I had my hat on when they took the photographs! Hallo, darling! We're alone!"

"You'd be surprised how often we're going to be alone on this trip," Mannering said.

Before Lorna could comment, before he could remind himself that at all costs he mustn't spoil this send-off, the old steward came along, smiling self-deprecatingly, announcing himself with a gentle cough.

"There are some flowers here for milady," he said. "And more *bon voyage* messages, also." He stood looking round, unable to find a space for anything more, even the one box of flowers and the smaller box, probably perfume, in his hands.

Mannering took them, the steward went off, smiling to himself, and Mannering said: "Coming on deck? Or are you going to open these first?"

"I think I'll have a breath of air," Lorna said. "It's stifling in here." She glanced at herself in the mirror again, and asked: "Will I do as I am?"

"Don't dare to alter a thing."

When they reached the deck, there was ample room at the rail. A gong was sounding, a little musical box tune.

"Luncheon," said Mannering. "We needn't rush."

They sauntered round the ship watching as she manoeuvred out of the docks as neatly as if she were a tiny catamaran and not one of the most modern ocean liners afloat. Dockers and workers, at the wharves and warehouses, watched with idle curiosity not untouched with pride.

"I don't know about you," said Lorna suddenly, "but I'm famished. Neither of us really had any breakfast. I hope the food's going to be good."

"I'll be surprised if it isn't," replied Mannering, hopefully.

They sat at a table for six, with companions for that meal only, and during it some of Lorna's high spirits left her. She looked tired, Mannering thought, and that wasn't surprising; she had hardly stopped working from the time they had decided to make the trip.

"You take a nap," he urged her. "I'll have a stroll round and find my way about."

"Don't leave me too long," pleaded Lorna.

He would leave her for hours, if need be, and she would probably drop off to sleep. Before he was out of the cabin she

49

was lying on her side, the bedspread over her, completely relaxed.

Mannering went up to the sun deck. Above everything he needed a little time to think; even to rest. He began to try to see the events of the morning in perspective; it wasn't easy. Larraby's call, the shock of seeing the broken vase, the astonishing appearance and behaviour of the two Chinese, the scene in the shop, the way Winchester had flung himself into the tackle—and there was so much more. The telephone calls, the note "You may leave the ship at Bombay. No later", the implied threat to smash up his antiques and the other things of great beauty at Quinns.

"We can do with a few days' quiet, and I suppose we ought to get it," he soliloquised to himself—and as he did so he heard footsteps.

They were familiar, and he had no doubt whose they were.

He turned to look along the great stretch of almost white boards, so scrubbed were they, and saw Lorna bearing down on him. Her coat was flying open and she walked so purposefully that he felt sure that this was not simply because she could not rest. As she drew near she took a small box out of her pocket and he recognised the *bon voyage* packet which he had thought contained perfume.

"Now what?" he asked, and tried to hide the flare of alarm that went through him.

"Now this," said Lorna. She handed him the box, and pulled him beneath the davits of the lifeboat, obviously so that no one else could get too close. They were in mid-river, and a long way from either bank.

Mannering opened the box.

A single ruby seemed to look balefully up at him from a bed of pale green velvet. It caught the sun and glowed, and it was almost true blood red. It was round in shape, so perfect that it seemed hardly real. Mannering had handled countless rubies in his time, but could not recall having seen one as lustrous, as red and as large as this.

"Some going-away present," he said, with feeling.

50

"It isn't a going-away present," said Lorna. All her high spirits and excitement had faded, and Mannering knew that his hopes of keeping her in ignorance of what had happened had been killed stone dead. "It's a welcome-home gift," she went on, articulating the "welcome home" very carefully. "Look."

She handed Mannering a card. It was plain white on one side, but on the other were typewritten words. Mannering felt sure they had been written on the same machine as the note to him. The wording read:

"Isn't it beautiful, Mrs. Mannering? This, and another like it, will be yours if you return to London within two weeks."

* * *

After that, Mannering had to tell Lorna everything.

He told her as she sat on the bed in their cabin and he sat on a chair with his feet resting close to hers. He left nothing out, and had no difficulty in recalling everything, so deeply had it impressed itself on his mind. Lorna did not once look away from him, and it was hard to guess what was passing through her mind. He still could not guess when he had finished. There was so little noise anywhere, and no movement of the ship. Suddenly, he was aware of tears filming her eyes, and he was deeply cast down, for he could imagine how acutely disappointed she was that those ghosts had visited them so swiftly, spoiling so much that was good.

"John," she said, in a choky voice, "why didn't you tell me?" When he made no attempt to answer, for there seemed so little to say, she went on: "Ask a silly question, deserve a silly answer. And you were right, my darling—I've had a wonderful day, a wonderful day. A whisper of this would have spoiled it, but—don't carry so much worry on your own. Whatever happens from now on, I must know. You'll tell me, won't you?"

Mannering answered very gently: "I'll tell you. Be sure of that."

Soon she was on her side facing him, knees drawn up, hair spread over the pillow. She wanted to talk, to speculate, to

51

know everything he thought. She was determined to make him talk, to bring everything out into the open, so that it was less likely to worry and preoccupy him. And inevitably she had to ask:

"John, what do you think we ought to do? Go back?"

He didn't answer.

"It's obviously the sensible thing to do, isn't it?" she persisted. "They've been good enough to let us go as far as Bombay, so we've nothing to worry about until then."

He still didn't answer.

"What good do you think it will do if we go on?" Lorna asked. "Any good at all?"

At last, Mannering said: "I don't know what good it will do, but I'm sure what harm it will do if I go back." He said 'I' deliberately, and with sufficient emphasis for her to notice.

"But darling!" she protested, almost hotly. "You've no obligation to anybody over this—not to Raymond Li Chen, or to Bristow, or to anybody. You'll be able to live with yourself, even if you do go back."

She knew exactly what was passing through his mind, and awareness of that forced a laugh from him.

"Let's not decide for a few days," he said. "If they really leave us alone until we reach Bombay at least we'll know there's a fifty-fifty chance of believing what they say. Think you can put it behind you for a few days?"

It was her time to laugh.

"I've been doing that for so long that it's almost second nature. How long have we got? A week?"

"A little more than a week, I'd say," said Mannering. As he spoke he heard the now familiar footsteps of the steward, and he looked at the notice behind the door: *Your steward's name is Wallace*. There was a pause but no tap; a little envelope was pushed beneath the door, and their name was facing upwards. The footsteps faded, while they stared down. Then without a word, Mannering moved across, stooped, and picked the message up. He opened it. There was a card about the same size as the one which had come with the ruby. He turned it over, and a moment later threw his head back and laughed—from sheer relief.

Lorna looked at him as if he had gone mad.

"Captain Cosford's compliments," he read, "and he hopes that we will grace his table for dinner tonight and throughout the voyage. Who said it had been a dull day?"

*   *   *

There was no message by radio-telephone that afternoon, and nothing happened to cause a moment's alarm. Much happened to cheer them up. Captain Eric Cosford, Commodore of the line, was a youthful-seeming middle-aged man, burly as a seaman's image, but with a ready wit, a gourmet's palate, and a genius for selecting the seven passengers to share his table. There were Sir George and Lady Wilde, both a few years younger than the Mannerings, going on to Australia for some diplomatic post that would doubtless soon be common knowledge. There were Mr. and Mrs. James Pargetter, Pargetter an American, and his wife Australian, who were in a big way in cattle and as big a way, if the first night was any guide, in fashion; and there was a rather older woman, the very gracious Miss Tenterden, beautifully gowned and beautifully groomed, obviously an old friend of the Captain.

"It's going to be a good voyage," Mannering said when they went to bed that night.

"It had better be," said Lorna.

In fact it was so good a voyage for the next few days that it was possible almost to forget the overhanging shadow. The sea was summer calm, the Suez Canal quiet and clear and strangely beautiful, the Red Sea not only bearable but pleasant with a gentle, cooling wind coming off the distant desert as they sailed past the land of Cleopatra, the land of frankincense and myrrh.

When they tied alongside at Karachi, all the camels and all the sorry-looking horses pulling their dilapidated *gharries* seemed to gather at the quayside. There was a great fuss about checking passports, but the formality took surprisingly little

53

time. The captain's table group, without the captain, wandered through the bazaars and the streets of shops, where voluble Pakistanis waited with patient hopefulness for trade. They finished the day at the sandy golf course for ice-cold beer, and reached the *Orienta* cheerful, content, and laden with mementoes—a dozen of them pencil sketches which Lorna had made and would treasure over the years.

There was a cable waiting in Mannering's cabin; from Bristow. It read:

"Nothing to report. Chinese prisoner has not said a word. Quinns flourishing."

"Only two days out of Bombay," said Mannering. "We can rely on another carefree twenty-four hours, anyhow."

But in twelve hours, when they were beside the swimming-pool, browned as only the Eastern sun can brown the European skin, clear-eyed, bodily as fit as could be, the carefree days came to a sudden end. A bar steward came up to Mannering with a marconigram on a silver salver. He caught a glimpse of Lorna, suddenly stilled in the middle of a smile, surprising Gillian Wilde. He opened it, and read:

"Far better to have two red rubies than to cry tears of grief."

7

BOMBAY

ALMOST as soon as the shadow of anxiety fell on Lorna's face, it lifted. She smiled at tall, black-haired Pargetter, and said something which set him and Gillian Wilde laughing, before she moved across, stepping over bronzed limbs and scarcely covered torsos, brightly coloured towels and gaily striped chairs, to join Mannering. It was too early for the sun to burn, so she wore no wrap; a bottle-green swimsuit showed just how magnificent her figure was, and young men as well as old glanced at her, some shamelessly, some covertly.

"Is it what we've been expecting?" she asked. Facing the calm ocean, she could afford to allow anxiety to show again.

"Yes." Mannering showed the marconigram to her.

"From London," she remarked, bitterly, "where nothing has been happening, according to Bristow."

"You forget there was a truce," said Mannering. "Now we'll have to make up our minds what to do. I'll race you four times up and down the pool, the winner to make the decision."

"Don't make light of it," Lorna protested, and yet relief began to show in her eyes. "You'd never let me win—and even if I won, you wouldn't do what I want you to do."

After a pause, while he quizzed her, aware that others were still watching her—and that two young girls were watching him with all the indications of hero-worship in their eyes—Mannering asked: "That depends. What do you really want me to do?"

Lorna did not answer at once. They had not talked about the situation since leaving London, although Mannering was sure that Lorna had thought about it quite as much as he. Now she looked at him with an expression which many would call sullen. He knew better. He could guess how her thoughts had vacillated, how she had tried to avoid being swayed by emotional fears, and how she had tried to see the situation as he did. She knew that; and she also knew that his greatest fear was for her.

"I suppose I know we'll have to go on," she said. "I wish to God it had never happened, but we can't pretend that it didn't. You want to go on, don't you?"

"I wish I could go on alone," Mannering said.

"Oh no, John. Not that. Either we both go home or we both go to Hong Kong." She spoke with such intensity that he knew she was afraid he would try to persuade her not to come with him. "Promise me that."

"Together, wherever we go," Mannering pledged solemnly. "Part of the time anyhow."

Alarm flared in her eyes.

"Don't hedge!"

"I've been thinking," Mannering said, mildly. "We needn't hand ourselves to these people on a platter. We may as well make them think we've got cold feet, even if we haven't. So if we disembark at Bombay, stay for a few days at the Taj, say, and then fly Air India or B.O.A.C. to Delhi as if we were going back to England, then fly to Hong Kong from Delhi, we'd get there in good time—and when we were not expected."

Now his eyes were beginning to crinkle at the corners, laughter sparking in them. Lorna thought how remarkably like her Cavalier portrait of him he was. "I could go on ahead— but not as the real me. The Wilmingtons will be glad to have you in Delhi for a few days, and we can soon work out the details. There are plenty of them."

After another long pause, Lorna spoke half amusedly, half exasperatedly:

"You'll have it your own way, whatever I say. You won't do anything definite without consulting me, though, will you?"

"Not a thing," Mannering assured her. "How about that race?"

Soon, she was breathless with exertion and with laughter. He marvelled, and was glad, and yet knew she also lived on the edge of fear.

*   *   *

Mannering sent a marconigram to Bristow, and a letter explaining in broad outline what he intended to do, and posted it on board; it would go airmail from Bombay. From the ship he cabled the Taj Mahal Hotel for a room, and cabled to the Wilmingtons, in Delhi: *Can you bear with Lorna and me for a few days next week?* If the captain's table was surprised by the change of plans, there was little comment. Mannering felt as if he were living in a state of semi-reality, suspended between his real intentions and his pretended ones.

The curious shipboard excitement, like a mild fever, touched nearly everyone on the night before Bombay. No one appeared to meet or watch the Mannerings. No one seemed to

56

notice that they went to a travel agency and booked passages for London with a stop-over at Delhi, and also went to a lot of trouble to get a refund for the unfinished part of the ship's voyage. It was almost disappointing—until they went into their enormous high-ceilinged room at the hotel, the air stirred by a huge ceiling fan as well as a breeze off the Indian Ocean which seemed to blow straight through the massive Gateway of India. A letter underneath the door was marked: *By Hand*. It could be from almost anyone, and they read it together:

"*The companion ruby is waiting for you at Quinns.*"

"So wherever we go we're watched," Lorna said.

"It won't be too long before we start watching them," said Mannering.

It was an empty thing to say, and both of them realised it, but it did one good thing: it forced Mannering to face up to the fact that they knew nothing at all about the people involved, the reason for wanting to keep him away from Hong Kong, and from seeing Raymond Li Chen's exhibition. He wasn't even sure that it had anything to do with Bristow's problem. If it had a political motive, there was no telling how dangerous it might become.

Was he right to take risks with Lorna? Was the wise thing to call the whole thing off?

He knew that if he did he would never be able to live with himself again, and that drove him to the obvious conclusion: he had to find a way to strike back soon. He had been on the defensive, almost on the run, for far too long. What he wanted to do more than anything else was to talk to Li Chen, and he put through a call to Hong Kong that evening. He stood by the window of the bedroom, watching the *Orienta* steam slowly out of the harbour and towards the open sea. The space by the Gateway of India was a seething mass of white-coated and white-dhoti'd men, gaily clad women and squirming, racing, laughing children.

His telephone bell rang. Lorna, sitting at the window, watched him as he moved towards it. Now he would have to decide what to say to Li Chen.

The operator said in sing-song English: "I am sorry, Mr. Mannering, but the gentleman you wish to speak to is not in Hong Kong today. He is said to be in London. Is there anyone else you wish to talk to?"

"No," Mannering said, through his surprise and disappointment. "No, thank you."

"It is my pleasure to help you, sir. No trouble." The operator rang off, Mannering shrugged his shoulders and remarked: "Li Chen has plenty of time to fly to London and back before the exhibition date, I suppose, but I've never known him visit London without advising the main dealers well in advance."

"John," Lorna said, "*he* couldn't be the man behind it, could he?"

"Why on earth should he be?"

"He may have started something which got too big for him, or he may have been frightened. It isn't any use going on to Hong Kong if he's not there, is it?"

"It doesn't look like it," agreed Mannering, but even as he spoke he argued with himself. It was easy to take it for granted that there was a connection between Raymond Li Chen's collection and the missing valuables from the Chinese mainland, but there was no possibility of being sure.

"Let's go for a stroll," he said. "I feel stifling." In fact he felt more frustrated than he could ever remember; whatever he wanted to do in this affair, he was forestalled or prevented. Even the seething mass of people in the streets, the continual babble of voices, the curry and rice vendors, the sellers of sweetmeats and cane-sugar pieces, of cigarettes and tattered books, of betel nuts and herbs and spices, could not raise his spirits. Beggar after beggar sidled up to him, keeping a wary eye on the nearest policeman. Each looked into his bleak face and moved away, discouraged. Then a tiny woman, with one child in her arms and another clutching at her sari, stood near with her palm outstretched. She looked as if she would do anything for the sake of a few *pice*. She actually blocked the Mannerings' way.

58

"John, give her something," Lorna said almost sharply. "Don't snap her head off."

"Do what?" asked Mannering, startled. He took two purple notes from his ticket pocket, and handed them to the woman— and as he did so, a small piece of paper slid as if by magic out of the folds of the ragged sari, and transferred itself to his palm. The little woman smiled, and her heart seemed to shine in her eyes. She murmured a word, and turned away. Mannering put the note in his pocket and walked on, looking about him. No one seemed to be taking any special notice of them, except the beggars, and one after another they stepped into their path, wary only of the police.

Many people were watching, and Mannering did not want to open the note yet, although he could hardly keep his hand off it.

They were back in the hotel before he took it out.

"You will find the woman who gave you this note near the entrance to the Jumna Temple", the note ran. *"Please come with her to see me."*

The signature was Raymond Li Chen.

*   *   *

"Is it Li Chen's writing?" Lorna demanded.

"I've seen it a hundred times, and I think it is."

"You can't be sure," Lorna insisted. "It could be a trick to find out if you're really giving the case up."

"There's only one way to find out," Mannering said. "By going to see him." When Lorna simply stood and stared at him as if astounded he went on quietly: "Darling, either we see this thing through, or we don't. If we do, there is bound to be a risk—but there have been a thousand risks in the past, and we're still alive and thriving."

"I know," Lorna said in a subdued voice. "When will you go?"

"Not too early," Mannering said. For a few moments they stood very close together. "Now the time has come to see if I

59

have forgotten the fine art of disguise. Care to hold the mirror for me?"

"You mean you brought your grease-paint case?"

"Of course I did," Mannering said.

Lorna forced a laugh, and picked up the mirror, but he was more troubled about her than he had expected to be. It was as if she had a genuine premonition of danger.

But soon she seemed to become as absorbed as he in what he was doing.

He sat in front of the dressing-table mirror, with a small make-up case open in front of him, and began to make changes to his face. He was adept as a man could be, and was utterly absorbed in the task. He created lines on his face which seemed to alter the shape of his mouth and nose and chin, worked the lines in until they seemed part of his skin. He aged in front of Lorna's eyes, ten or fifteen years at least. He worked on his hair, and his eyes so that they looked narrower and smaller, and he worked grease-paint into his nose so that it looked reddish-blue and veined. Time passed so quickly for each of them that when at last he finished, they were startled to find that it was nine o'clock .

"Will I do?" asked Mannering. His voice didn't sound like his own, but that of an American, rather hard with broad vowels—Bostonian and Harvard, most people would have guessed. "It's a lucky thing I brought that seersucker suit." The suit was of striped black and off-white cotton, cool and beautifully tailored—a suit bought for a heat-wave in New York a year before. He put this on. Out of a pocket in the lining Lorna took a small peaked cap of matching material with flap at the back, and a pair of rather new-looking tan brown leather brogues. He put these on, and stood up.

"I hate to say it," Lorna said, "but no one could possibly recognise you."

"That's what I like to hear, hon!"

When Mannering left her, she was smiling; and that represented no mean achievement on his part.

He listened at the door for a moment, heard nothing, and

stepped outside. At the far end of the tiled passage were two white-clad floor waiters, consulting earnestly over trays. They looked up when he approached.

"Good evening, *sahib*."

"Good evening, sir."

"Hi," said Mannering. "How do you get out of this place?"

They escorted him along the corridor, which matched one on the other side of an enormous well, towards the lifts. An attendant took him down. The hallway was nearly empty, more staff than guests stood about idly. Mannering walked out by the main entrance and across the gardens, ignoring two taxi-drivers who tried to catch his eye. He walked briskly in the cool, starlit night towards the Gateway; stars reflected on the calm water. Most of the crowd had gone, but the beggars and the food vendors were still there; it was like running a gauntlet of eager, voluble auctioneers. He walked towards the heart of the city until he was sure that no one followed him, then hailed a passing taxi. It was a Mini-Minor, and the driver was a huge Sikh wearing a turban, but dressed otherwise in European clothes. His English was excellent.

"Jumna Temple, sah. I know that very well, very famous place. All my life I am knowing Jumna Temple.... The American gentleman is in a hurry?" He shot the little car along the cobbles, swaying from side to side. "I am very fast driver, also very safe. Not once in all my life have I had a fatal accident while driving...." He swerved wildly to avoid a motor cycle. "Son of a wanton, do you wish to break my life-long record?... American gentleman could not choose a better taxi-driver in all Bombay. I know it like the palm of my two hands. Also I tell fortunes. Also I take gentleman for night-life tour?... Perhaps you think no night-life in Bombay, ha! ha! ha!... American gentleman is indeed wrong. Wonderful night-life, beautiful women, Oriental music, Western music, the Blues, the Twist, also the Beatles, we have them all. One hour tour for gentleman?"

"We'll see," said Mannering. "Stop by the temple, will you?"

61

"Temple not open all night, sah, but very good to see from outside. I take gentleman from America..."

They pulled up outside the temple. Mannering thrust three rupees into the driver's hand, but the man stretched across, held the door, and looked and sounded as if he were astounded and affronted. "For one hour tour, twenty rupees, gentleman."

"I've taken a ten minute drive," Mannering said. "Keep the change!"

He watched the taxi drive off swaying as if with its driver's wrath, into the dimly lit street. This was a very different part of Bombay, with tiny shops, still open, and shady side streets, flickering oil and candlelight, pale electric lights, people looming out of doorways and standing or squatting still and silent. Across the road were the shapes of the towers of the temple, and of holy men squatting by it. A woman with a baby in her arms and a child clinging to her dark red sari was standing as if with the patience of Job.

No one appeared to take any notice of Mannering, yet a thousand eyes were watching, a thousand retinas had the image of the tall man in the pale, striped suit. He approached the woman, who hardly came up to his breast, and she put out her hand in automatic supplication.

Mannering took the signed note from his pocket, unfolded it, and handed it to her. The way her eyes rounded in surprise was the best proof possible of the effectiveness of his disguise.

"Take me to the man who gave you this note," Mannering said.

She nodded, but he did not know whether she understood the words or simply the implication. She turned with a rustle of cotton, and the toddler by her side clung to the old and tattered sari and trotted along with her. They passed men sleeping in their bundles of rags, and others squatting and staring as if silently, yet Mannering knew that those thousand eyes were turned towards him.

Soon, he would know if the summons had really come from Raymond Li Chen.

62

8

THE MAN IN THE SHADOWS

THE woman and her children made no sound; it was as if Mannering was following ghosts. *Ghosts.* The woman turned into a narrow street which had no pavements, only the cobbled roadway which went close up to the walls of houses and of shops. A few glimmering lights broke the darkness, that was all. Now he fancied he could hear the faint padding sound of the woman's footsteps.

She turned into a doorway, and disappeared. He moved to follow her, but a man stood in the doorway—an Indian in a *dhoti* which made him, too, look like a ghost. He did not speak, but pointed to the right.

Mannering looked round. In another doorway, standing still, was a shorter man in a pale western-style suit. Mannering could not see him well because of the poor light. He stood in shadow.

Mannering said: "Thank you," and crossed towards the second man, who did not move.

Mannering stopped in front of him, controlling his expression, keeping his voice low. The man was undoubtedly Chinese, but was not Raymond Li Chen.

"Do you know Li Chen?" Mannering asked.

"Me not know," the Chinaman said in pidgin English.

"Tell him I want to see him," Mannering said. "I am John Mannering."

"Me not know," the other insisted. "Ask other man, please." He pointed along the street, and Mannering turned and peered through the gloom, but saw no one. He looked back—at empty shadows. The Chinaman had gone, as silently as the woman and her children.

The night was still. Only the stars lit the street, which was both eerie and frightening. He did not go away immediately, but the seconds grew into minutes and there was no sign of anyone whom he had seen. He went along a few yards, to a tiny shop where several men squatted on either side of a metal bowl on which steamed some white-coloured mess, no doubt with a rice base. He asked:

"Do you speak English?"

None of them answered.

Mannering was less afraid than annoyed, and almost angry. It was as if he were fated to fight shadows. An open menace would be better than this uncertainty.

A man appeared by his side; it was the Chinaman.

"You not Mr. Mannering," he said clearly. "Who are you?"

"I am from Mannering," Mannering declared, knowing that it would be folly to betray his disguise to anyone whom he did not know. "Take this to Li Chen." He took the invitation from Li Chen from his pocket, and the other took it without a word, and walked away; he seemed to be swallowed up in the gloom.

The odour of curry and other spices wafted along the alley; and the stink of sewage, too. Slowly Mannering became aware of the drone of distant traffic, in that other world so nearly the real West. His ears and eyes were strained. It was easy to imagine that every tiny window and narrow doorway, every roof and every corner, had watching eyes.

There was a stir of sound, and the Chinaman reappeared.

"Please come," he said; it sounded like "Plees clum". He turned his back on Mannering, who hesitated only for a second, and then followed. Such moments as these were the moments of greatest danger. If he had walked into a trap, at least he would soon know. He saw his guide disappear into one of the doorways; once he himself was inside, a trap could close on him. He went in. There was a rustle of movement ahead, and a pale light coming through a brass lantern with many holes; a Tibetan lamp. Beyond this was a plain wall, with pieces of plaster broken away, and wide cracks in it, like huge spiders squashed in while the cement was still wet.

The Chinaman opened a door, and stood aside, now he was very polite. Mannering held his breath as he stepped through

64

the doorway. Beyond, over an alcove, a different kind of lantern hung, spreading a different kind of yellow light; a Chinese lantern. Mannering went beneath this into a room which was different from any he had seen for a long time. This was Chinese; square stools and silken cushions, rich carpets and lacquered tables showed that it was the home of a wealthy man.

Raymond Li Chen stood in front of a glass showcase.

* * *

Mannering had no doubt at all of the man's identity; he had seen Li Chen too often to be in doubt; the last time only a year ago. He had a fine, broad forehead, and a gentle expression, quite puzzled now. He was tall for a Chinese, five feet eight or so. He wore a gown which reached to an inch or two above the tiled floor.

"It is not possible that you *are* John Mannering," he said.

"It's not only possible, it's an indisputable fact," Mannering retorted in his natural voice. "How are you, Li Chen?"

After the first moment, the Chinaman's face lit up, the smile touching his eyes as he moved forward, right hand outstretched. As they shook hands, he asked:

"But why are you in such a disguise?"

"For the same reason you sent a beggar woman instead of coming to see me yourself."

"That is reasonable, I suppose." Li Chen took Mannering's arm and led him into a smaller room, just as unmistakably Chinese, but with upright chairs and a waist-high table. He clapped his hands lightly, and motioned Mannering to sit down. They waited. Mannering knew better than to interrupt. Soon, a little woman came in, also wearing a Chinese gown. She smiled up, as if shyly, across the tray she carried. Tiny handle-less cups were on the tray as well as a teapot. Ceremoniously, she set the tray before Li Chen, and left the room as silently as she had come.

The men sipped. Mannering waited for the other to speak.

"There are some who wish to stop you from going to Hong

Kong," Li Chen said at last. "They believe they have succeeded." After a pause, he asked: "Have they?"

"Who are they?" countered Mannering mildly. "Do you know?"

"I am not certain," answered Li Chen, quietly, "on the one hand it could be the Peking government; on the other hand it could be the Nationalist government on Formosa. Each government is interested in some goods I have in trust for others. I do not know whether it makes much difference, Mr. Mannering. Whichever it is, they will use any means to achieve their objective." He spread his hands, palms towards the floor. "I came here to India because attempts have been made to frighten others, who live here. I hoped to find out who was responsible, but so far I have failed. Of course whoever it is will make sure that no crime can be brought to their door. You have a picturesque phrase for my position, Mr. Mannering—between the Devil and the Deep Sea."

Mannering did not correct him.

"Are you sure it is one government or the other?"

"If you say to me, can I prove my contention—no, I cannot, hard though I have tried. If you ask me whether logic or reason or even the law of probability could put the blame on anyone other than a government, the answer is no. It is a long story, although I can soon tell you enough to help you to understand. First, Mr. Mannering—what are your plans?"

"To visit your exhibition in Hong Kong," answered Mannering.

A smile dawned slowly on the Chinaman's face, and it seemed to be one of pure satisfaction. As he looked into Mannering's eyes, his own were bright and gay.

"Thank you very much. They have not frightened you then?"

"Not enough to keep me away."

"But a little, I see." Li Chen paused, but soon went on thoughtfully: "Is Mrs. Mannering afraid?"

"Yes, much more than I."

"How great a value there is in honesty," approved Li Chen.

"So you left the *Orienta* in order to make these people believe you are too frightened to proceed—and it seems you have succeeded. What do you intend to do? Fly from here to Hong Kong as an American—such a very convincing American." The Chinaman added that as if it gave him a great deal of satisfaction.

"I haven't tried to deceive an American yet," Mannering demurred.

"I know many of them, from all parts of the United States and no two are the same, and yet all of them have an indefinable quality which marks them as Americans to everyone else. You have that mark, as well as an unmistakably American voice. But that should not surprise me, knowing so much about you as I do. You will fly, yes?"

"When I see you in Hong Kong I'll tell you what route I took," promised Mannering.

"Such very great caution—and such wisdom, also. Mr. Mannering, I waited in Bombay to see you in this secrecy because of two things. I am myself now in very grave danger, and whoever assists me will be in equal danger. For myself, I will run any risk that is necessary, but I do not wish to jeopardise the lives of any friends."

The quietness of his words gave them an effect greater than any vehemence would have. Mannering felt sure that this man meant exactly what he said, and in those few simple words he had contrived to say a great deal. All of that was underlined by the cloak-and-dagger manner of their meeting, and by recollection of the strange, dark streets outside.

"What risks are you running?" asked Mannering.

"Death," Li Chen answered simply.

"Why should you be in danger of murder, and who is likely to kill you?"

Li Chen moved forward, poured out more tea, and took the lid off a delicate-looking jar, which he proffered to Mannering; it was full of golden brown biscuits which looked as fragile as procelain. Mannering took two; they melted in his mouth. He took two more, but Li Chen did not touch them.

"For many years I imported precious things from China," he told Mannering. "Some were technically smuggled, but money was paid to the Peking government. I had talked to many Chinese officials not only in nearby Canton but also in Peking; in both these places I was received as a welcome guest. This so-called smuggling was known to and tolerated by the government. Currency from outside the Communist area is difficult to obtain, and China needs to buy much more than she can hope to pay·for by exports. The money demanded for these goods was always sterling, Australian pounds, Swiss francs, German marks, or Canadian or United States dollars. With so many business associations I had no difficulty in making the payments in those hard currencies, and the British authorities raised no query. There are few import regulations in Hong Kong. I am, you understand, a British citizen by birth, and also I am a man of repute. We live in a strange half-world, where we must do things which by some standards are dishonourable but in Hong Kong are not only acceptable but most praiseworthy."

He paused, as if to allow Mannering to murmur: "No one knows that better than I."

"You are most kind," said Li Chen. "You wish to ask a question perhaps?"

"Yes. You said that some of these goods were supposed to be smuggled, and the authorities closed their eyes to it. What about the rest?"

"The rest was bought in Hong Kong, from Chinese government agencies," Li Chen answered. "However, this has been a time of unrest on the world markets. There were many side-effects from the assassination of President Kennedy, and there has been great reluctance to spend money on goods which might be confiscated."

Mannering echoed: "Confiscated?" and the emphasis betrayed his surprise.

Li Chen spread his hands in that now familiar gesture.

"No citizen of the United States may import into his own country any goods which are manufactured inside Red China.

68

This ban is absolute. It applies particularly to works of art, which so many Americans wish to buy. Some have bought them in spite of the ban, and have obtained forged certificates of origin attributing the source of the goods to other parts of the world. Others bought them and stored them against the day when the ban would be lifted, as they all believed would happen one day. I have two storerooms in Hong Kong which is a treasure house of such goods, held in trust for American clients. Most reputable dealers have such storerooms. So the volume of the trade has been very great—three, four, five million pounds a year is common. Now——" Li Chen broke off.

"Don't the Chinese need the hard currency any longer?" asked Mannering. Much of what he had been told he knew already, but he had never realised how tight a stranglehold it was on trade.

"I cannot read their minds," Li Chen said simply. "I only know that the Peking government has declared the smuggling of goods an offence against the nation—treason. It is retrospective, also. I have been accused of buying goods knowing them to have been stolen. I, who had tried so hard to be neutral, to help both sides, to keep open the channels of trade between East and West—a vital need, Mr. Mannering, one which is absolutely vital."

Mannering nodded: "I know. Did they accuse you openly?"

"Oh, yes," answered Li Chen. "A complaint was made to the governor, but he refused to believe it. It is good that a man should have such friends. I am in no danger from my Hong Kong friends, but listed among the goods now said to have been stolen are many which are in my warehouses, some my own, some held in trust. In fact I was planning an exhibition of them, as you well know—and I truly believe it would have been the finest and the most valuable collection of Chinese and Oriental art ever to be displayed. For such an occasion I dared to ask you to come, and also many others whom I knew would be enthralled by what they saw."

"I can well believe they would," said Mannering. Questions were seething in his mind, but he forced himself to wait.

This time Li Chen seemed sunk in contemplation for a long time: it was hard to think of anyone less like a man living in fear of his life. He was very grave and gentle-voiced as he went on; the only hardness about him was the light in his eyes.

"They cannot compel the authorities to act against me, so they have come direct to me. Their agents have told me that unless I return the collection, all of the collection, whether it is mine or whether I hold it for trust for American citizens, they will kill me. And if that were not danger enough, there is more from the Nationalist government—or its agents—in Formosa. They say that the treasures are in fact theirs, that I must surrender everything to them, under pain of death. So to save my life I need two treasure houses, filled with these wonderful things. You understand what I mean when I say that I am suspended between the Devil and the Deep Sea?"

9

THE DEVIL AND THE DEEP SEA

Li Chen spread his hands again, gave a self-deprecating little smile, and clapped his hands. The woman glided in with fresh green tea, and with a bowl of steaming meat on a silver tray. She put these down on the table between the two men, bowed, and disappeared, making only a faint shuffling sound. Mannering had a mental image of the wizened old woman's face of the mother and the two children who had led him here, but the vision soon faded into the greater one, the terrifying dilemma in which Raymond Li Chen found himself.

"The Devil and the Deep Blue Sea," Mannering mused, not realising that he had slipped in the "blue"; nor did Li Chen appear to notice it. "I know exactly what you mean." He had another mental picture—of Lorna's expression when she heard about this. She would cry out in dismay and alarm: "Don't you get involved, whatever you do don't get involved." And how right she would be.

Li Chen picked up the salver, and on it were ivory chopsticks as well as two long silver forks. Gravely, he offered the dish.

"A Chinese delicacy," he explained. "It is what you would call roast duck."

Mannering picked up a fork; he was in no mood to handle chopsticks. He speared a piece of the duck, a rich appetising morsel, and ate it; the flavour was delicious. Li Chen used chopsticks with negligent ease, finished the mouthful, and then said:

"Perhaps you will change your mind now and return to London. Undoubtedly that would be the wise as well as the only safe course."

"Undoubtedly," agreed Mannering drily. "How did you know where to find me?"

"It was not difficult, Mr. Mannering. I received your kind letter saying that you and your wife would accept my humble invitation, at the time that I was first threatened by these men of violence. Immediately I telephoned Quinns, hoping to catch you before you sailed. I understand from Mr. Larraby that I had missed you by a few hours. He told me what had happened—and also that your Scotland Yard had become involved in the investigation. He further told me that your ship would be at Bombay. I wanted to see my old friends here—you will remember Old Phirozha? His daughter and her husband now control the shop he left to them, and they do much business with me. Attempts were made to keep them away from Hong Kong, also. I have an uncle who has been an exporter of teas and spices for many years. This is his house." He took another piece of duck. "I came by air, secretly. The Hong Kong police are guarding my shops and my warehouses, at the moment only I personally am in danger. I telephoned you on the ship but was told you had disembarked. I was about to telephone you at the Taj Mahal Hotel, but my uncle's friends told him that some Chinese from Peking were also staying there, so I took these extra precautions." The Chinaman smiled. "I know enough about you to be sure you would not be troubled by such methods. I confess I did not expect you to be able to make me so anxious. Even as I look at you, I find it difficult to believe that you are John Mannering. You look as if you are an American—a New Englander, I would say, on vacation."

"That's one good thing." Mannering smiled, but his eyes were bleak and very thoughtful. "Are you in danger then, here?"

"I am in danger wherever I am."

"Have you been attacked or threatened here in Bombay?" insisted Mannering.

"No, not here," answered Li Chen. "But at my uncle's place of business there have been inquiries for me—no threats, you understand, simply men who ask if I am in Bombay. Who would be interested, Mr. Mannering, except my enemies?" He placed another piece of the duck in his mouth, ate it and went on: "I telephoned you in London hoping that I would be able to stop you leaving. If you need a holiday there are other, safer, places for you to go. This is none of your business, Mr. Mannering, and none of your responsibility. I am sure your wife would agree."

"I'm sure she would, too," said Mannering drily. "Who knew that I was coming to see your exhibition?"

"Many people," said Li Chen. "It was reported in the *Hong Kong Tiger Standard,* a piece of gossip, you understand. So all of Hong Kong may know. Why do you ask?"

"Someone was very anxious to try and stop me," Mannering pointed out. "I'd like to know why."

After a pause, Li Chen said almost blandly:

"I was anxious to stop you, and I still am, because I do not wish you to submit yourself to such danger. Your reputation is very great, Mr. Mannering, and widely known. There are inquiries which the police and the authorities can make, but it is

72

possible that you can probe farther and in a different way. From the point of view of either Peking or Formosa it would be much better if you were not active in Hong Kong. You see, neither government will ever admit that it is exerting pressure on me. These men of violence, these gangsters, are paid by government agencies, but that is difficult to prove. In the East, authority often closes its eyes. The Hong Kong authorities will go so far and no farther. They are in a very precarious position, and they must cause no offence either to Peking or Formosa. But you, an individual of such rare ability—you might find *proof* of the connection between these men and their government that their guilt can be proved and the Hong Kong authorities would not be able to ignore such proof. So you are not wanted in Hong Kong by anyone, Mr. Mannering."

"Except by you."

Raymond Li Chen shrugged.

"I have now advised you not to come to Hong Kong."

"But if I find this proof of the source of the threats, proof which no one else will look for seriously, it would help you."

"The ways of the East are often called inscrutable," Li Chen said. "In fact they are very simple and sensible. If proof were available, if I could say to either government that its guilt could be proved, it would withdraw."

"Can you be sure of that?"

"A withdrawal would avoid loss of face. It would also avoid a crisis with the Hong Kong authorities, and therefore a crisis in London."

Mannering said slowly: "I see." And in fact there were some aspects which he saw very clearly indeed. If Li Chen's assessment was right, and it sounded irrefutable, this was a delicate issue, encroaching on politics and diplomacy. Something which could cause a spark could cause a conflagration. No one wanted that. Li Chen might well be sacrificed to expediency, but few people would be any the wiser.

He was this man's friend, but did that warrant him taking

73

grave risks not only with himself but with Lorna? Everything he had heard made him want to shy away from this affair. The odds were too heavy, the cause not really his. He might, in fact he did, feel almost as if it would be a betrayal of Li Chen if he backed out, but that was an emotional reaction and there was no justification for it. All of this passed through his mind as he looked into the other man's eyes. Was it imagination, or was there a shadow of both understanding and disappointment in them?—as if Li Chen had read his mind, and knew exactly what he would decide.

He asked abruptly: "When will you go back to Hong Kong?"

"I am not sure, my friend."

"Is it safe for you to go back?"

"It is not exactly safe for me to go anywhere. Mr. Mannering, will you answer me two questions, and give me the benefit of your advice? Such a problem as this demands the wisdom of Solomon. Would you, if you were me, attempt to come to terms with both governments? Would you, in all these circumstances, feel bound by honour to protect the goods which are held in trust for American friends? Remember that although there is insurance on the goods for which exit permits from China are available, some cannot be insured. In any case it is not possible to cover even the legitimate goods to their full value, which fluctuates from time to time. The Americans would lose much money, and they would lose possessions on which they have set their hearts. You know how collectors feel, Mr. Mannering. No one knows better than you." Li Chen stopped again, and offered the salver, as if he were deliberately allowing Mannering time to think.

"No thanks," said Mannering. "How can I get in touch with you?"

"You mean here in Bombay?"

"Yes."

"I can give you this telephone number, but you should be very careful how you use it." Li Chen shrugged. "Here in India, as anywhere in the East, it is easy to buy information.

In the West this is called corruption, but ways and customs and ethical standards are very different."

Mannering nodded. "I know." He knew it both as a fact and as an excuse, but did not think about it much. "Would you rather I gave a message to the woman?"

"Woman?"

"The beggar."

"Oh, I understand," said Li Chen. "I think it would be wiser, unless perhaps I telephone you. But what will you wish to discuss, Mr. Mannering?"

"Whether to go home, or to continue the journey," answered Mannering. "I need a day or two to think."

"Mr. Mannering, there is no need at all to study my feelings or to soften the blow of your return."

"I want time to think before making up my mind," Mannering said. He wanted to telephone Bristow too, and to decide how much of this to talk over with Lorna. He went on: "And I need time to think before answering your questions, too."

"You must have as much time as you need," Li Chen said graciously. "Mr. Mannering, may I hope you will stay and dine with me?"

"I must get back to the hotel," Mannering refused. "Thank you all the same."

"It is my loss," murmured Li Chen. "I will arrange for you to be escorted to the temple. From there you will be able to get a taxi."

"I can find my way," Mannering assured him.

He was almost brusque, and knew that this was because he felt exasperated with himself, his own indecision, and the fact that Li Chen was right and was fully aware of it. He was playing for time so as to let the Chinaman down lightly. Nothing could possibly justify taking any further part, and yet deep inside him there was a voice crying out *to* take part. The truth was, he wanted to. It was not that he thought he should, conscience had nothing to do with it. He responded to such a challenge as this as other men responded to the call of the high mountains, or the great oceans, or great causes. It was the

75

same call which had made him the Baron. There was one reason only why he did not decide on the spot to go to Hong Kong: and that reason was Lorna.

Could any man ask for a stronger or better reason?

Li Chen saw him to the door which opened on to the narrow alley. The combined odours of spices and sewers wafted strongly from the corner. With a quiet: "I will expect word from you soon," Li Chen closed the door, as if afraid to keep it open too long. A man moved across towards Mannering out of the shadows, and his heart bounded: if Li Chen had cause to fear, then surely he had, too.

The man was his guide.

They walked towards the wider street, past the dim lights and the squatting figures and the unseen eyes, and reached the corner. Somewhere reedy music was being played, high-pitched and melancholy. Mannering saw the lights of cars in the distance, and had only to walk to them to find a taxi.

"I can manage on my own from here," he said. The guide hesitated. "Go back," Mannering insisted, and pointed. Still the man hesitated, but he allowed Mannering to walk on alone. The music seemed louder: *ding, dong, ding, dong,* quite tuneless to him; and yet very sad.

He heard a different sound: a child's crying. He should not be surprised and yet he was; one seldom heard a child crying, or even whimpering, in this city. He heard it again, and then in the dim light from a shop where no one sat or stood, he saw the child. She was standing against a wall. By some trick of reflection her dark eyes were shiny and huge in a pale face.

She whimpered.

She, thought Mannering, and realised on the instant that it was the child who had clung to the beggar woman's sari.

There was no other sound.

He stared at the child, wondering if this was some kind of trick, meant to keep him here, or to make him anxious. He was in India, remember, there was no room for sentiment, for poverty and distress was part of life; no one man could alter

76

that. This was a land of organised beggars, trained from the age of this very child to trade on human sympathy, to make a business of begging.

He took a coin from his pocket and held it out, but the child did not move a hand; she whimpered more. Then, his eyes more accustomed to the gloom, he saw a dark bundle on the cobbled ground, a few feet away from the child. He stepped nearer. It was not a bundle, it was a prostrate body, curled up as if asleep. Worse: only a few inches from the body was a baby—the baby which had been in the woman's arms.

Mannering felt the cold clutch of horror as he called: "Wake up." The woman did not stir. "Wake up!" he repeated and stretched out a hand. The woman's wizened face was just visible, and now it was obvious that she was lying in an odd, unnatural position. He drew back, took out a book of matches, and struck one.

He started back, appalled, for the woman's head was a mass of hair, matted with blood. Blood was red on her cheeks and slimy on the cobbles where her head lay.

The match burned low, and died into darkness, and the awful sight was hidden. Slowly, Mannering straightened up. He felt sick with shock and with horror, and with a dawning fear. Had she been murdered so that he would find her here? Her body lay across his path like an immovable barrier between him and Hong Kong.

A hand touched him and the child whimpered, while the babe lay still as death. The shadowy guide said in English that was difficult to understand: "Go. Pliz go." He was pointing towards the temple with his other hand, and what Mannering could see of his expression seemed to plead urgency. "*Go. Pliz go.*" He, Mannering, must run away, he must not get involved in this. For a few seconds he stood still. Then in a sudden surge of anger he shook the urgent hand away, threw back his head, and called:

"Police! Police!"

Almost like a wraith his guide vanished, leaving Mannering alone with the dead woman and the whimpering child. He called again but the only response came from the child who, frightened, began to cry quite loudly.

"Police!" shouted Mannering, but there was no answer and no new sound. He looked about him, trying to see if anyone approached, but even the silent men who had squatted on their haunches seemed to have gone, leaving the street empty, eerie, frightening.

Then there was a shuffle of movement, and Li Chen's guide appeared again.

"Police will come soon," he stated. "Master telephone."

On the last word, he vanished into the gloom.

10

THE ORPHAN

IT seemed a long time, but at last a car turned from the main road into this one, a car engine whined, and tyres rumbled over the cobbles. Headlights shone on Mannering and the dead woman and her children. No one else was in sight. A youthful man in uniform jumped out of the car, approached Mannering and saluted.

"Did you call for assistance, sir?"

"I certainly did," said Mannering, in the accent which had fooled Li Chen.

"I am sorry you have been inconvenienced in Bombay," the police officer apologised with great precision. "We do not like such a thing to happen to guests in our country. Where are you staying, sir?"

"At the Taj Mahal Hotel."

"If you will please be good enough to explain briefly what happened here, sir, I will take control of the situation and my superiors will call at your hotel for further formalities. What is your name, please?"

"Mason—James C. Mason," Mannering said. "You're very helpful." He had already made up his mind what to say. "I had been told there was an antique shop near here—do you know what I mean?"

"Perfectly well, sir. There is such an establishment not far from here. No doubt you were misdirected. What then, sir?"

Other policemen were bending over the body, and suddenly a light flashed vividly and a camera clicked. Above Mannering's answer there was a strange sound, and suddenly the child by the wall screamed in terror. A woman appeared, old and crone-like, her heart touched and compassion overcoming her fear. The other policemen spoke to her, and she took the child. She pointed to the body which lay so still, and the policeman near the dead woman answered in Hindi; Mannering did not understand a word.

"What was that?" he asked the officer.

"The woman and the infant are dead," the officer stated flatly. In the light from the car headlights he showed up clean-shaven, handsome, not so dark-skinned as many. His eyes were very dark and bright. "You were about to give me further information, sir."

"The woman approached me as I walked here, and I gave her five twenty-anna notes," Mannering said. "About half an hour later I came back, heard the child crying, and found the mother dead."

"If she is the mother," the police officer said sceptically. "We do everything we can to prevent it, but it is still possible to hire children, the better to solicit alms. What followed, Mr. Mason?"

"I called for help but no one came, and then raised my voice and bellowed," Mannering said. "No one answered. I was surprised to see you come."

"You were heard," the officer told him. "A man telephoned to say that an American gentleman was in some difficulty. We were alarmed in case you had been attacked and robbed. Every city has districts where it is unwise for a stranger to travel alone by night." There was no doubt of the note of reproof.

79

"Sure they have. Who'd walk in Central Park, New York, after dark? It was my own fault, lootenant, and I'm sorry."

"I am also exceedingly sorry. In future you will please be more careful."

"You bet I will," Mannering assured him fervently. "How can I pick up a cab?"

"It will be my privilege to drive you back to the hotel," the police officer said formally. "I will instruct my assistants to wait for me."

It had been a mistake to say where he was staying, Mannering realised, but he was not worried about that; he was troubled about the child who had been taken into one of those dark, mysterious houses.

"What will happen to the kid?" he asked as he sat beside the police officer in the old Austin.

"She will be cared for." The man obviously had no desire to discuss the subject. "What is your room number at the hotel, please?"

Almost mechanically, Mannering answered: "Eighty-one." In fact his was 307. "Will you do me another service, lootenant?"

"If it is in my power, sir."

"Drop me by the statue by the big arch—what do they call it?"

"The statue of Lord Hardinge of Penshurst, sir, close to the edifice known as the Gateway of India. You prefer to go there instead of the hotel?"

"Sure," said Mannering, and added with a note almost of longing in his voice: "I guess that must be about the most romantic harbour scene in the world. I just love it."

"Truly it is a beautiful place," the officer said with obvious pride. "It will be my pleasure to take you there."

Ten minutes later Mannering stood and watched the little car drive off from the shadow of the huge gateway. Almost as if by magic, two children and a woman with a babe in her arms approached him in silent supplication. He pictured the young–old face of the woman who was dead, and the bright

80

dark eyes of the orphan, and for a moment he was nearly blinded with tears. He thrust money into the dirty palms, and turned and strode away, walking for ten minutes along the great promenade with its circle of lights until he was fully composed again.

Then he went back to Lorna.

*　　　*　　　*

"By far the worst thing was that child, crying," Mannering told Lorna, huskily. "I've never heard anything like it, and I hope I never will again. What I can't understand is *why*? Who thought it worth while killing that harmless creature? Could it have been to frighten me? Who could think that it would be enough to frighten me away, anyhow?" He sat at the mirror, talking as he cleaned off the make-up; the real Mannering appeared, the man "Mason" vanished. "It was a damnable thing to do. A hideous thing. You can see that can't you?"

"Far too well," Lorna agreed.

Mannering half expected her to go on, but she did not. While he was applying solvent to the gum in the corners of his eyes, he continued: "Li Chen sent for the police, of course. He could hardly do less. My God, what a mess he's in!"

Lorna said in an even quieter voice: "Yes, isn't he? And he wants you to stay away from Hong Kong."

"Only a fool would go there now," Mannering growled.

"Why didn't you give him his answers on the spot if you feel so strongly?" Lorna asked, and there seemed an acid note in her voice.

"I don't know what I would do in his position," Mannering said, gruffly. "Would you try to do a deal with both governments? Neither of them can have everything it wants, and one or the other probably won't be satisfied with half. As for what to do with the goods he's holding for the Americans——" Mannering had his eyes screwed up while the solvent gradually loosened the gum, and that way his face was twisted as if he were in pain. "What would I do in the same circumstances?"

81

"I know one thing," said Lorna, and undoubtedly her voice was very sharp. "You wouldn't have to ask a second opinion on that. You would protect them more than you would if they were your own, you would have only one meaning for 'in trust'."

"I'm not so sure," objected Mannering. "Any American who buys goods made in Communist China knows he is taking a risk, and pays Li Chen a storage charge to take the worst of the risk. No, I'm not at all sure that I know what I'd do."

"Let's have a drink, and think about it," Lorna suggested, more mildly. "You're not seeing it clearly yet, you're too upset by the woman's death. Shall I order a snack, too?"

"Good idea," agreed Mannering. "And we'll put a call into Bristow's office. It's not much after six o'clock in London, he'll probably be there."

They were subdued for the next half-hour, and whisky and soda, with some wafer-thin sandwiches, didn't help. Mannering kept on recalling aspects of the talk with Raymond Li Chen, trying to put himself into the other man's shoes, but it did not make the issue any clearer to him. He was soon on edge for the call to London to come through. It was nearly a quarter past twelve when the bell rang, and he jumped up so quickly that he nearly spilt his coffee. A girl said: "Your call to Superintendent Bristow in London, England, sir." Almost at once Bristow's voice sounded, crisp and clear.

"Now what's your trouble, John?"

"No trouble yet," Mannering answered, "but there could be plenty. Bill, why did you ask me to have a look at this case?"

"You know very well why," replied Bristow.

"I've reason to doubt, as I always had," declared Mannering. "Why wasn't it easier for the Yard to deal direct with the Hong Kong police? Had you—or had they—any reason to pull punches?"

Lorna was watching Mannering very closely.

After a long pause, Bristow spoke in a less assured voice:

"Now what kind of reason would you think we might have for pulling punches?"

82

Lorna looked almost as if she understood what Bristow was saying, and all the implications of question and answer. Mannering looked straight into her eyes as he answered: "There could be several reasons. Political go-slow methods, for instance, a delicate situation in which officialdom must sit on the fence but plain John Citizen may jump down on either side, if he's fool enough. Perhaps he'd never get up again. Give it to me straight, Bill. Lorna's with me, remember. I don't want to risk her neck even if I risk my own."

"I should think not," said Bristow. "Give me a moment to think."

It grew into a long moment, and during it Mannering told Lorna what he had said; she needed no telling that if Bristow needed time to think, it was tantamount to admitting Mannering was right.

Finally Bristow said: "John, you could be doing us a very great service by finding out the truth. You can't find it out without risk. That's as far as I can go, but if you do get to Hong Kong, Police Commissioner Brabazon will tell you more. If you don't go, you won't need to know more. Understood?"

Slowly, Mannering answered: "Yes, I think so. Thanks."

"Any time," said Bristow. Then he appeared to regret the flippancy, for he added in a more serious voice: "Give my love to Lorna."

He rang off, the last words echoing in Mannering's ear. They had come so clearly and so loudly that he thought Lorna had probably heard them. He saw her lips move, forming "Love to Lorna indeed". Mannering put the receiver down, but did not move away from it. He took out his cigarette case. Lorna struck a match for him, and watched the flame die down, as she often did. Once again Mannering had a swift, mental picture of the cruel sight—the bloodied back of the woman's head, the orphaned child's eyes strangely bright and bold, yet somehow fearful, in the flickering light of a match.

He drew deeply on the cigarette.

83

"No one will make up your mind for you, will they?" Lorna said. "You've just got to do it yourself."

Half smiling, and with smoke curling out of one corner of his mouth, Mannering asked:

"Won't you make it up for me?"

Slowly but quite positively Lorna shook her head.

After they had gone to bed Mannering lay awake long after the moment when Lorna began to breathe deeply in sleep. One window was open and he could just see the stars, which looked close and bright—like the matchlight on the eyes of that bereaved child. It was still easy to hire children as aides to successful begging, the police officer had said, but he was not convinced in this case. The way that child had clung to the sari had made him think instinctively of them as mother and child. What would happen to the mother and her infant now? Burning on one of the funeral *ghats,* the bodies devoured in the leaping, crackling flames, far out of the pain, the hunger and the fears of the world, as well as robbed of its light and its hope. The living child would now be put out to hire so as to touch the hearts of the simple and the generous. What could he do about it anyhow? He was Mannering, not Mason; if as Mannering he showed any sign of interest in the child the police might suspect the truth, and if they began to question him closely and to probe, he might not be able to leave Bombay for days. Give the police any reason at all to suspect him, and they would worry him, terrier-like, until they felt they knew the truth.

At last he went to sleep. He did not dream.

When he woke it was full daylight. The sun did not strike the window but seemed to strike the sky, tinging its blue with gold. He glanced at Lorna, and saw her looking at him, half smiling.

"Sleep well?" he asked.

"Fine, yes. Did you?"

"Better than I expected," he admitted. "Better than I should have done, I suppose. What a beautiful morning. Like some tea?"

84

"Soon," said Lorna. "Darling——"

He did not quite know what to make of her, and it was not often her mood puzzled him. He said: "Hm—hm?" and waited.

"I've made up your mind for you," Lorna said with great deliberation. "In two ways—I mean about two things." Mannering felt his heart begin to pound, and also felt the words "no, don't", spring to his lips. Even with her, his mind was his own. But he kept silent, and she went on: "If it weren't for me, you wouldn't think twice about going to Hong Kong, and I've always wanted to go there. Why should I let you be so over-protective that I have to stay away?"

Now his heart leapt, but he lay quite still.

"And the other thing is about this child," Lorna went on. "Do you remember selling some Indian jewellery for the Oxford Committee for Famine Relief? It had been given by Indian donors in England, and you didn't charge commission."

Mannering made himself say: "I should think not."

"We had a letter from a Mrs. Patel Chandri, who serves on the Committee here. I'll go and see her today, and tell her I'm representing a Mr. Mason, an American friend who wants to keep out of the picture. I'll ask her to make sure the child is properly cared for, and we'll see it doesn't cost anyone any money. Will that do, John?"

"How do you know Mrs. Chandri's still here?"

"I didn't tell you, I'd forgotten, but when I told Lucy Pleydell we were calling at Bombay she asked me to try and see Mrs. Chandri, who is still very active in good works over here."

"There must be a thousand opportunities a day for people to do good works," Mannering said, very humbly. "Are you sure about Hong Kong?"

"Quite sure."

"Then I know how to advise Li Chen," said Mannering almost flatly. He did not want to show his feelings too much. "I'll tell him that if I were in his shoes I wouldn't try to come to terms with either government, I would do my damnedest to

85

prove they were involved, and so make them call off their dogs. And I would honour the trust the Americans put in me—I'd protect that treasure as long as I breathed."

"There's my John!" Lorna's smile had an ineffable quality. "I would hate you to be anything but yourself for me."

*   *   *

Mannering felt as if the very air was ambrosial; he had never felt more deeply in love.

*   *   *

With the decision made, the way to implement it opened almost at a touch. Mrs. Patel Chandri, middle-aged, plump, gracious, sari-clad, was delighted she could help. During the day she telephoned Lorna.

"We have the child in a private home of worthy people, Mrs. Mannering. Such sadness there has been for her, but she will soon forget. Also, the police have found the murderer, who attacked her mother for the little money she had, and killed her because she screamed."

Mannering felt a sense of deep relief; at least he was not responsible for what had happened, unless he could blame himself for being generous with her.

Raymond Li Chen said simply, on the telephone:

"I feel shame that I ever hesitated, Mr. Mannering. If you come to Hong Kong, I will show you that I will not hesitate again, although I cannot pretend that I will not be afraid."

The Wilmingtons, in Delhi, submerged them with hospitality, and tried hard to make them stay.

Instead, James C. Mason, with a false passport and some substantial American Express Travellers' Cheques, flew on the same aircraft as Lorna to Bangkok, then left her with friends at the British Embassy while he flew ahead to Hong Kong. She had fewer fears for him as James C. Mason.

11

THE ISLAND OF JEWELS

"HAVE you ever been to Hong Kong before?" inquired the stewardess, who was young and charming and very English. For some reason she had taken a liking to James C. Mason, possibly because he was one of the two unaccompanied men on board; this had proved to be a family flight.

"No, ma'am, never in my life," said Mannering. "I've been most places, but not to Hong Kong."

"I hope you like it," said the girl.

"Why? Don't you?"

She looked at him frankly, and there was a dreamy expression in her eyes; they reflected the blue of the sky which stretched out of sight in all directions.

"I love it," she said simply. "It's like an island of jewels by night as well as day."

Several passengers who heard her, stared. The steward came along and broke the spell by saying they were approaching land. The "Fasten Belts" sign began to flash over the cockpit door, alternating with "No Smoking". Mannering fastened his belt, and the stewardess checked it; she used a perfume like attar of roses and had a complexion like Dresden china.

"You can see the island now," she said.

It was indeed like a jewel, close to the great, sprawling mass of the mainland. Pale mist rose from the sea but the sun struck the hills and the buildings on the island and the myriad of ships in a harbour which seemed to grow and glow. There was a kind of iridescence, many colours of subtle hues, and as they drew nearer inlets into the island and the mainland showed, crammed full of ships which looked so tiny, and also looked as if they had come from another world.

A man leaned across to Mannering.

"We land on the New Territories," he vouchsafed know-ledgeably.

"Look!" a woman said from behind them. "There's Red China!"

As far as the eye could see there was Red China, and in sight was the border across which so many jewels were smuggled.

There was more than the usual hustle and bustle on board as they approached the airfield; there was real excitement. This was dimmed only a little when the customs authorities, some Chinese and some English, proved very thorough, although hardly a thing was dutiable here. Mannering wondered why they took quite so much trouble. The excitement was damp-ened a little more because the taxis looked so dilapidated, and so many Chinese were in Western dress. It was not until they were driving through the streets of Kowloon itself that a sense of excitement came back. Great banners with Chinese lettering hung and swung from the narrow windows of new buildings and of old, and huge lanterns hung with the colourful washing on a thousand poles jutting from a thousand windows.

"This is Nathan Road, sir," announced the driver. "Penin-sular Hotel, just round the corner. Hong Kong island is across the water."

"Yes, sir," said the Chinese receptionist, "we have your cabled reservation.... Yes, sir, there is a room with a harbour view.... Will Mrs. Mason be coming today?... Later, sir, I quite understand." Keys jangled and porters hovered, lifts worked slowly, and deposited Mannering on the seventh floor. White-clad servants stood by an open door at the end of a long wide passage, another was waiting inside the large, high-ceilinged room with two windows overlooking the incredible blue of the harbour which was seething with large and small craft, junks and sampans and modern catamarans, warships, and cargo boats and a great, white-hulled ocean liner.

"You want something, please?" asked the white-clad man. "I your room boy, you tell me."

"Fine," Mannering said, and realised on the instant that he

had used his English-speaking voice, so great was the effect on him. "Later," he added, and slurred the "t".

"One thing remember, please." The "boy" made it sound almost like "lemember". "Water very scarce Hong Kong, one hour morning, one hour evening. Bath full now, no more till six o'clock."

It was now half past two.

"I'll remember," Mannering assured him.

"Velly good, sir." The boy, who was fifty if he was a day, bowed himself out, and the door closed.

"I must shake myself out of this," Mannering said aloud. He unpacked one suitcase, then opened a map of Hong Kong which he had studied on the aircraft. This was Salisbury Road, and he had to turn left out of the hotel, then left again into Nathan Road to reach the shopping district of Kowloon—where Raymond Li Chen had his main shop; he had a smaller one on Hong Kong Island. Mannering went out, taking the city map with him, read street names and found his way without difficulty. The shops were on the right, behind a façade of new hotels and office buildings, but with some older shops as well. The pavements were crowded with bustling people, mostly very slight and small; shop after shop was crammed with curios. He saw more ivory carvings, more jade and more costume jewellery in the course of half an hour's walking along narrow streets and through modern arcades than he had ever seen in one place before.

"I should have been here years ago," he told himself, but it was only a passing thought. "Won't Lorna rub her eyes!" He laughed in anticipation, the danger which would also surround her almost forgotten.

He came upon a corner shop near Mody Road. It was built in the apex of a triangle of narrow streets, and had long windows along each side, but this did not explain the sudden change in his manner. The contents of the window did. There was a Ming vase, duck-egg blue in colour, which was almost identical with the one which had been broken at Quinns. Next to this was an ivory set of an emperor and his empress carved

89

so exquisitely that only a master could have done it. On a shelf, near these, were some green jade vases, each almost unbelievably beautiful in shape and carving.

It was almost incredible to find so much together in one place.

He looked up to the facia board and read: *Li Chen Brothers: Works of Art.*

Inside the shop was a woman in a high-necked gown of sapphire blue, and an elderly man in European dress. Mannering knew they were aware of him, but they concealed their interest. Little men stood near most shop doorways, ready to invite visitors in, but no such touting was permitted at Li Chen Brothers.

Mannering stepped inside. The woman waited until the door closed behind him before coming forward. She was not young, and yet there was a look of youthfulness about her, in spite of the lines at her eyes and the corners of her mouth, which looked like hairline cracks in precious porcelain.

"Good morning, sir. Can I help you?"

"I'm just looking round," Mannering said. "A friend recommended this shop to me, he told me I could rely on getting good value and genuine works of art here."

"That was very good of him." There was a slight lilt to the woman's voice. "I am sure we shall justify his confidence in us. Please do look at everything you wish, and take what time you need. If you require help, please call on me."

"Why, thanks." Mannering nodded, smiled, saw the oldish Chinaman smiling at him gravely, and began to move around the shop. It was quite dream-like here. Year after year he had seen the Li Chens' catalogues, yet he had never pictured such variety, such excellence, such quantity. In this one shop there must be two hundred thousand pounds' worth of *objets d'art.* Ivory, jade, turquoise and rose quartz carvings filled a dozen shelves on a dozen showcases.

He moved back to the woman, empty-handed.

"It is too much to take in at one visit," he said fervently. "I've never seen such a display anywhere."

90

"You're very kind, sir."

"The Ming vase," Mannering said. "What period is it?"

"The seventh, sir, the Dynasty of Lo Ming. There are only four such vases in the world. One is in the Mellon Gallery in Washington, one in the Guggenheim Museum in New York, one is in the shop of Quinns, in London. And of course, this one."

"How much is it?"

"In Hong Kong or American dollars, sir?"

"American dollars, I guess."

"Fifteen thousand four hundred and fifty American dollars, sir. But there is one thing I must tell you. I cannot give a certificate of origin to satisfy your customs regulations. It is genuine, you understand, and was made in the China mainland."

"I know the difficulties," Mannering said. "There's no chance of smuggling it in, either. Is Mr. Raymond Li Chen in?"

"I am sorry, but he is away on a buying mission. Mr. Charles Li Chen will be glad to help you—Mr. Raymond's brother."

The elderly little man who had kept so silent and so still, looked up with another smile. He came forward, and at the same time the door at the back of the shop opened, and a girl appeared, with tea and tiny cups on a decorated *papier mâché* tray.

"I am Charles Li Chen, sir."

"When will your brother be back?"

"In a few days at the most," the Chinaman replied. "He is to return here for an exhibition which it is proposed to hold in our Hong Kong Island galleries. You have perhaps heard about that?" He poured out tea, and offered little golden brown biscuits from a porcelain jar.

"Sure, I've heard about it," Mannering said. "Thank you." He sipped. "I certainly hope to come and see it. My name is Mason, and I'm from Boston."

"I am glad to know you, Mr. Mason. Please come here as often as you like, without obligation. I hope that——"

91

He broke off, and his courteous expression changed to one of alarm. Mannering spun round. A small car was passing, and a man was standing up in it and hurling something at the window—a small, round, dark missile, which might be a rock or might be a grenade. It crashed against the window. A great star appeared, spreading from the centre of the glass. The woman went forward with bewildering speed, and Mannering saw that she was making a desperate attempt to protect the Ming vase. Two men ran past the window, as if to chase the little car. Charles Li Chen went towards the door. The glass did not shatter and did not fall, and the missile hit the pavement and rolled harmlessly into the gutter. The woman now stood between the window and the vase, like a hen protecting her chicks.

Then two things happened at once. Charles Li Chen, in the doorway, suddenly went flying, and two men appeared in his place. They wore peaked caps, low over their eyes, and European clothes which were too big for them.

One of them pulled a hammer from under his coat, the other a length of iron piping. The woman cried out in Chinese, but her tone was unmistakably one of anguish. The door at the back of the shop opened and another man appeared, elderly, scared-looking. He was no match for the raiders, and even had he been, even if he put up a good fight, hundreds of the precious things in the shop would be damaged, and most destroyed.

Mannering remembered the way the Chinaman at Quinns had eluded all the assistants. Each of these men might be just as difficult to catch, and even more willing to smash that vase. He did the only thing possible; pulled the automatic from his pocket and fired into the floor at the feet of the two men. The report rang out, making Mannering's ears ring. The men, who had ignored him until then, started back. Their weapons were raised, fear driving away their determination to smash everything within reach.

"Out," said Mannering. "Quick!" He fired again. One of the men jumped backwards, the other dropped his hammer and raised his arms as he also backed towards the door. "Get a move on!" Mannering roared. "Out!"

Charles Li Chen, on his feet again, moved towards them quickly, and kicked each behind the knees. They crumpled up. Outside, dozens of people had already gathered, mostly Chinese but with a sprinkling of European, and as Charles Li Chen bent over the raiders and delivered chopping blows on each man's neck, two policemen appeared, uniformed and armed.

The woman was moving across the shop to Mannering, and there was a film of tears in her eyes.

"It will never be possible to thank you, Mr. Mason—never. And it will be impossible to say how grateful I am."

"Mr. Mason," said Charles Li Chen quietly. "Whatever we can do for you, we shall do. Please command us."

"Are you Mr. Mason?" one of the policemen asked, with a kind of polite aggressiveness. Two more had arrived, and were marshalling the crowd outside.

"That's right," said Mannering.

"Would you mind showing me that gun, sir—and your permit to carry it?"

*　　　*　　　*

The police station was like police stations the world over; this one was one of the old ones, with small barred windows and narrow passages. Most of the men on duty were Chinese, but two of the three in the room with Mannering were English, one of them in particular was the like of Bristow, but a taller, more massive man. The other was dark-haired and on the plump side; he looked as if he could find it easy to smile but wasn't smiling at the moment.

"So you've no permit for a fire-arm, Mr. Mason?"

"No, sir."

"Did you declare your gun at the customs house?"

"No, sir."

"Why didn't you?"

"I didn't think I'd be allowed to retain it," answered

Mannering, frankly. "I always like to be able to protect myself. If I hadn't used it in the shop there would be a lot of porcelain fragments instead of works of art."

"That's as may be, sir," said the man who was like Bristow. "Nevertheless it is a serious offence, and we shall have to confiscate the gun. Had you declared it openly you could no doubt have obtained a permit."

"I've heard that story before," said Mannering. "I don't think it would have been so easy, either. Are you telling me I can't have it back?"

"I'm afraid not, sir."

"Where do I apply for a permit?"

The dark-haired man had rather small, speculative-looking green-grey eyes. The other's eyes had a cold glint in them.

"How long do you expect to stay in Hong Kong, Mr. Mason?"

"Maybe a week or ten days."

"Do you seriously expect to need a gun in that time?"

"I've needed it once already," Mannering retorted. "What would be so surprising if I needed it again? I carry a lot of money around with me, and I might buy some valuables here, including jewels. Is that an offence in Hong Kong?"

"No, sir. If you will send a written request for a permit I'm sure the Superintendent will consider it quickly. You will hear about the offence already committed in due course."

Mannering said: "I guess it's no use arguing. I'm sorry about the offence, but I'm glad I had that gun. So is Mr. Li Chen."

"No doubt at all about that, sir," said the Bristow-like officer. "How well do you know Mr. Li Chen?"

"As well as you can get to know a man in ten minutes flat." The time would come when he would have to tell the police who he was, but it might not be for days. He wondered whether a British licence for a gun was good in the Colony; he would soon find out.

Twenty minutes later he was entering the huge lounge of the Peninsular Hotel, no longer agog at everything he saw, but asking himself the question he could not answer. Had the raid on the shop been sheer coincidence, or had it anything to do with his visit? He could hardly believe it had; and when he thought back, it seemed to him that Charles Li Chen and the woman had been on the look-out for it. Before long he must talk to them, but that did not necessarily mean he would be told the truth.

He walked towards the lifts, and then missed a step, for Christiansen of London was sitting and drinking tea at a window table. He was alone. And he had said he was not coming to the exhibition.

12

THE DEALERS ARRIVE

MANNERING walked between the red-plush tables in the huge room, towards the window, to make sure that he was right. It was undoubtedly Christiansen, a blond Norwegian who had lived in London since the war, and was one of the most reputable as well as the most knowledgeable dealers, and yet a man whom Mannering had never really liked. For that matter, he had never really got to know him. He went on to the lift. There was no reason at all why Christiansen should not change his mind; in any case, there had been no obligation on him to tell Mannering whether he had intended to visit Hong Kong or not; he might have assumed that Mannering's question was a feeler.

Mannering went up to his room. One of three floor boys on duty moved from a table, unlocked his door, and stood aside, half smiling, half bowing. Mannering stepped into a sunlit room. On the dressing-table was a small packet. He had ordered nothing and expected nothing, but it was addressed clearly to him. It was the size that his gun might make, if it were packed in a box. He chuckled at the thought; if he ever got that gun back it would almost certainly be on his way out of the country. The packet was firmly sealed with plastic tape. He weighed it up and down on his hand, and found it very light. Was there any reason at all to be suspicious of its contents? He decided that there was not, prised an edge of the tape up with a penknife, and tore the rest off. It was a box with a lid. He took the lid off and found cotton wool, like soft snow. He pulled the top layer off carefully, and stared down at a miniature model of a Buddha, beautifully carved in turquoise, eyes and nose, chins and folds of his gown, all exquisitely shown. He picked it up, slowly, responding to it as he did to all beautiful things. Then he saw the card in the lid of the box, picked that up, and read:

"Again, a thousand, thousand thanks.
Charles Li Chen."

"Well, that didn't take them long," he reflected aloud. He carried the Buddha to the window, and the daylight gave the blue an even greater sheen; how Lorna would love this! The man or the woman in the shop had heard him telling the police where he was staying, of course. He seemed fated to be able to render the Li Chen family a service. He wondered again, uneasily, if the raid on the shop could have been coincidence; he simply did not know what to think of that, but was quite sure of one thing. The stock in that single showroom was enough to make the average dealer drool; it was impossible to imagine what the main galleries would be like when everything from the storerooms and warehouses was on show.

Would everything be brought out for display? After this desperate attempt to smash so much, would the Li Chens risk the rest? If the attack had been made by the hirelings of one government or another, though, would that prove to be anything more than a token act of vandalism? How would it serve either government if the treasures were destroyed?

"It must have been just a warning," Mannering said aloud, and the telephone bell rang on his words. The instrument was

96

on the table between the two beds, and he moved across, putting the little Buddha on the pillow of the bed nearer the wall, where Lorna would sleep when she arrived in two days' time. A lot could happen in those two days.

"Hallo. Who's that?"

"There is a cablegram for you, sir. I am checking to see if you are in."

"A cable for me?" He was surprised. "For James C. Mason?"

"Yes, sir, that is the name."

"Send it up to me, will you?" Mannering rang off, frowning. Larraby did not know the name he was using here; as far as he was aware, no one did. He waited impatiently until there was a light tap at the door, and when he opened it one of the room boys was holding out an envelope. "Thanks." Mannering took it, closed the door, and opened it. A single glance at the signature told him what he wanted to know: Lorna. But it was not really from her, for all she said was: *"This just arrived quote 'Ho partners flying to exhibition. You contact Commissioner Brabazon in emergency, Bill B.' end quote Love Lorna."* Mannering's thoughts carried him back to the luncheon meeting with Bristow and the curio and antique shop on the corner of that old London street. There was nothing really surprising in the fact that the Ho partners were on their way, but Bristow obviously thought he should know, so there might be grounds to suspect them of complicity.

He put the cable on the dressing-table, and looked out of the window. The sun was setting and there was a grey-blue haze over the harbour waters and the craggy island with its mass of buildings. A row of lights leading to the top of the island showed faintly against the glow, like a lighted stairway to the sky. He felt the fascination of the island taking fresh hold of him, and when he heard a tap at the door he thought impatiently: why don't they stop pestering me? Then he realised how unjust that was; he hadn't known service like this anywhere for a long time. He called: "Come in," and moved towards the door. This time a white-suited boy he did not

97

remember came in, smiling very broadly, almost nervously; a second boy followed, bowing so low his face was hidden.

"Water on now, we run bath," the first man said, and made a beeline for the bathroom, with the other trotting on his heels. This was certainly service in the old tradition.

The first man suddenly spun round. Mannering saw his right hand move, a moment later his wrist was gripped so tightly that pain shot through his arm. He felt himself thrust back against the second man, whose hands were suddenly clapped over his mouth, warm, clammy hands which seemed to choke the breath out of him. It had happened so quickly Mannering hardly had time to feel fear, but fear rose in him. The hands were taken away, and sticking plaster was slapped over his mouth and nose; he could not breathe properly, he could not call out. He kicked at the Chinaman in front of him, but his ankle was grabbed and he was pitched backwards. Breathing was so difficult that he began to fear that he would not be able to draw enough air in, that the plaster would suffocate him. He tried to breathe gently, but his body was subject to such convulsive exertions that he could not. He could not even gasp. His lungs seemed to become full and tight, and to swell up so that the pressure against his ribs brought a new agony. This was how it would come, this was the approach of death. In those few seconds he actually believed it, but he still tried desperately to breathe through his one clear nostril, which the plaster did not cover.

He felt himself lifted by the shoulders and by the ankles, and carried off quickly, but he did not know where they were taking him until they lowered and then dropped him, and water surged all about him.

This was the bath, half filled with water which lapped about his body and his face, and trickled into the nostril which was his lifeline. He must struggle, must kick out, must free himself. But if he struggled, he might drown himself; he must keep still. He felt hands at his wrists and feet, and realised that they were being tied together, but still he dared not resist. He saw the close-cropped hair of one of the men close to his

98

face—very thin, nut-brown hair; he could not see the other man. He felt the water trickling down his throat, and swallowed with painful care. Then the man straightened up, the yellowish face was very close to his, a round face, a short nose with wide nostrils, narrowed eyes—the face of a million Chinamen. Suddenly this man picked at the plaster and cleared the other nostril, and for the first time since the attack he felt the fear of death recede.

They left him.

It was a long, narrow bath. The back of his head rested on the slope at one end, and the soles of his feet at the other, keeping only his face clear of the water. He dare not even move enough to look down at his body and his legs, if he did he would disturb the water, and the danger was already too acute. He lay absolutely still. There were sounds of traffic outside; and there were closer sounds, in the bedroom. He had no idea what the men were doing, and did not greatly care. All that mattered was that they should not come back in here. For a while there was quiet, and he thought that they had gone, but suddenly he saw the top of the door moving.

The two men came in together, both smiling—as if they were really amused. One of them came forward very quickly, stared down at him, and then slowly stretched out his hand and nipped his nostrils together.

The fear of death flared up again as Mannering's body heaved. The pain at his lungs became almost unbearable. The dark eyes were close to him, the expression on the yellow face made it look as if he were relishing every moment of this; as if he were gloating over his victim.

He released Mannering's nose, but kept his hand hovering above him, then began to lower his hand very slowly. Mannering clenched his teeth and drew in all the breath he could before he felt the fingers pinch as if they were made of steel. No Chinese torture could be more refined than this. Could he hold his breath long enough? Did they mean to kill him? There were the two of them, staring down at him. The grip was tighter, painful in itself, and there was no way in which he

99

could stop himself from heaving; the top half of his body was out of the water. His lungs began to pulsate as the breath in them rushed to his mouth and tried to find an outlet; his body heaved and heaved again. There was a reddish mist in front of his eyes, and through the mist he could see Lorna's face, as clear and life-like as if she were in the room with him. That was when he was sure that he was going to die.

He felt his senses fading as his body was convulsed.

Then he was jerked out of the swoon by a sharp pain at his mouth. He did not know what it was, only that there was a tearing sound. All at once his lips were open, air rushed into them and seemed to burn his throat. Now his heart began to beat with a furious throbbing, and that in turn threatened to choke him. He felt his legs churning the water, and his head bumping against the enamel of the bath. His eyes were open all this time, but the figures looming over him were blurred, the round faces were shapeless, the teeth seemed to be chattering, big and simian.

Gradually his vision cleared and his heart steadied and his body relaxed. He was alive, not even badly hurt. The faces above him became those of men, and now he remembered he had seen one of them before, at Li Chen's shop—this was one of the two raiders. If it were necessary to use the same man for two attacks, increasing the risk tenfold, then it surely meant that the other side was short of manpower. That was his first coherent and logical thought since the attack. He mustn't forget it, the significance might be vital.

The man he recognised was squatting on the edge of the bath; he was the one who had pinched his nose. His lips were parted, and he looked rather as if he were smiling, but there was nothing to suggest amusement in his berry-brown eyes. He appeared about to speak, but stayed silent for so long that Mannering wondered if he were thinking up some new form of torture. Then in a voice with a curious clacking note in it, he said:

"Mr. Mason, where you come from?"

"The hell with you," Mannering made himself say.

He did not really want to; he hated to risk another ordeal. But if he gave in too easily it would probably seem unconvincing. He had to steel himself to hold the other's gaze.

"I ask once more, Mr. Mason. Where you come from?"

"And I'll tell you once more—the hell with you!"

The questioner did not move. The other man did, shifting slowly towards the foot of the bath. Each of them took his time, whatever he did, as if the slowness of their actions was part of the means of persuasion; and so it was. The man put his hands on Mannering's ankles, and without a sound he began to pull Mannering forward. As his ankles and feet rose out of the bath at the foot, so his head began to sink, until water lapped over his face, his lips, his nose. He kept his body rigid. If he struggled it would be too ready a sign of defeat, but——

His resolve broke.

Why was he tormenting himself? Why didn't he give them some answers to their questions? Any answers, anything which would make sure that this torment stopped. He managed to raise his head out of the water, and to gasp:

"All right, all right, I'll tell you!"

The man at the head of the bath pulled him back into position, and as he did so, Mannering went on chokily:

"I'm from Boston, Massachusetts. That's in the United States, I'm a United States citizen."

"Very interesting," the spokesman said. "You are a friend of Li Chen?"

"I've never seen Li Chen, never been in that shop before, if that's what you mean."

"Then why you act so quick?"

"That's the way I do act, that's me all over. I'm used to looking after myself, I could see you were going to smash that Ming vase. That would have been a crime, you understand? One hell of a crime, I had to stop it. You——" He stopped short, realising too late what he had done: he had told this man that he had recognised him from the raid at the shop, and therefore would have no difficulty in recognising him again. "I

101

came here to see the exhibition, I was told it would be just great, and if the goods in that shop window are typical it will be the greatest."

"Are you a collector of such things, Mr. Mason?"

"Collector? I'm a dealer. I run my own little business, buying and selling. I came here to look over what Li Chen's got to offer, and I know what my customers want. If that stuff didn't come from Red China I could sell most of it back home. There are some collectors in Boston who are crazy about Chinese works of art. Now you tell me something: why did you try to smash that vase? What has Li Chen done to annoy you? It's a crime, and I don't just mean it's against the law, I mean those things are unique, it's a crime against society, against art, against——"

"Mr. Mason," the man interrupted, "are you a friend of Mr. John Mannering, from London?"

The question came without any warning, so phrased and so unexpected that Mannering was tricked into showing astonishment. He covered that quickly; astonishment could be caused by more than one thing, even the change of subject might explain it. But if this little devil of a man forced the question it might be difficult to convince him that he was telling the truth.

"No," he muttered. "I'm not a friend of Mannering. I've seen him once, as a matter of fact, when he came to Boston. He's got a branch there. He——"

"Mr. Mason," the little Chinaman interrupted again, "it would not take long to drown you, you understand; not very long at all. Tell the truth, please, quickly. Are you a friend of Mr. John Mannering?"

The man at the foot of the bath gripped Mannering's ankles again, and exerted enough pressure to give menace to the threat. Now Mannering began to wonder if they had discovered anything in the bedroom which might have given him away, whether there was any point at all in lying. Almost at once another thought brought an even greater flare of alarm: whatever he told them, would they leave him here alive?

102

Would they risk being identified? Would murder worry them, or would they kill him as deliberately and slowly as they had already drawn him under water?

If he hesitated for too long, that would be suspicious; if he simply denied being a "friend of Mannering" they might disbelieve him. What had Li Chen said? "Between the Devil and the Deep Sea."

Mannering was staring at the nearer man, still not decided, when a thudding sound came not far away, followed by a crash as of breaking wood, and another thud. The two men sprang to their feet and swung towards the door, as the crashing and the thudding continued.

Someone was trying to break down the bedroom door.

13

ONCE A POLICEMAN...

MANNERING could not move because his wrists and ankles were tied; the best he could do was keep his head above water. The strain on his neck made even that difficult, if he had to stay in this position for too long, it would be impossible. He was completely at the mercy of these two men. They could turn him round, push his face under water until he drowned; or they could use a knife; or they could bludgeon him about the head. He saw a bludgeon in one man's hands, knobbed, murderous-looking.

It was the one who had raided Li Chen's.

The thudding and the banging continued, the floor shook and the walls reverberated. It lasted only a matter of seconds and yet to Mannering it seemed like hours. What would they do? His mind was split between the glory of hope and the dread of death. Then the man with the bludgeon jumped forward, out of the room, talking in that clacking voice, like a human Donald Duck. Mannering had no idea what he was saying but they were both out of the bathroom, they were leaving him unhurt. He craned his neck even more; there was a streak of pain from the back of his head halfway down his spine, but it did not prevent him from watching.

The first man flung up a window; the second climbed through it, nimble as a goat, and the other followed. That wall was sheer. The only hope they had was to climb from window sill to window sill, and if they slipped it would be the end. He saw a pair of legs dangling, and realised that they were going upwards, to the roof.

The legs disappeared.

Another, louder crash was followed by a short, groaning kind of quiet; then footsteps sounded, of men running into the bedroom. An Englishman called out:

"The window!" After a flurry of footsteps he and two Chinese policemen appeared at the window, and one of the Chinese began to climb out. Other footsteps followed, and a man glanced into the bathroom. On that instant the strain at Mannering's neck became too great, and he sank down. Water surged over his mouth and nose, he gulped, and began to choke. He struggled convulsively for a moment, but stopped when hands touched him firmly, and a man said sharply: "Stop jumping about!" He lay still as the speaker gradually raised him up, so that not only his head but his shoulders were above water. There was so much water in his eyes that he could not see clearly, and the water in his ears made it impossible to distinguish the voice, but he was raised gently out of the water, right out of the bath, then carried into the bedroom and put down at full length on a bed.

The danger was past, and he could breathe freely again.

He felt the cords at his wrists part. Pins and needles began to prickle through his hands and forearms, but not enough to harass him much. The cords at his ankles were cut next. Someone dried his head and face with a towel, and his vision as well as his hearing cleared enough for him to recognise the face and voice of the English detective from Police Head-quarters who looked so like William Bristow.

*   *   *

"There's no reason at all why you shouldn't know what happened, Mr. Mason," said the detective. "We didn't believe your story, particularly the explanation of your chance visit to the Li Chens' shop. A lot of peculiar things have happened to the Li Chens lately, and a number of American citizens have been trying to get their goods out of his store, where they don't think they're safe. We think you went there to try to remove your own goods, or on behalf of someone else in the United States. We're very interested in Li Chen's business, and we don't like armed robbery or violence anywhere on the Colony. So we had you watched. When you came up to your room we felt that you were safe enough, but in fact the two assailants came in by the staff entrance, overpowered the floor and room boys and tied them up, leaving them in a service room. They were traced by another boy who came looking for them, and the alarm was raised. I think you can consider yourself lucky."

"The luckiest," Mannering said, fervently. "Just one thing, Captain——"

"Chief Inspector Lovelace."

"Just one thing, Chief Inspector. I don't know a way of telling you how grateful I am."

Lovelace grinned. In fact he was not only bigger but better-looking than Bristow, and his eyes crinkled attractively at the corners.

"That's what Charles Li Chen felt about you, according to his statement. It's becoming quite a chain of gratitude. I'm glad I could help, but I was just being a policeman. There's one thing you can do to say 'thanks' and show that you mean it."

"What's that?"

"Tell me the truth about your presence in Hong Kong."

Mannering looked at Lovelace levelly, but did not answer at once. He was now sitting in an armchair, with a lightweight

105

dressing-gown over pyjamas. He was pleasantly warm, and but for the burning sensation at his wrists and ankles and soreness at his mouth and nose, he felt well enough. He had seen himself in the mirror. His upper and lower lips, almost to the nose and chin, were puffy and spotted with globules of blood where the plaster had been pulled away so roughly, but there were no other outward evidences of the ordeal. As far as he could judge he was still more like James C. Mason, in appearance, than John Mannering. Lovelace did not seem to doubt that he was an American, which was the best possible tribute to his accent.

Lovelace shrugged. "Well, I can't make you tell me, but you'd be wise for your own sake as well as Li Chen's. Think it over, will you?"

"Sure," said Mannering. "Don't get sore, Chief Inspector, I've good reasons for keeping my own counsel. I've a message of introduction to Commissioner Brabazon, and I'll present that today and talk to him. I imagine he will want me to talk to you immediately after that."

"You couldn't be the F.B.I., could you?"

"No," said Mannering, "I couldn't." He smiled. "But I could be a man who needs a fire-arm."

Lovelace laughed. Judging from his manner, nothing was likely to disturb his composure, and there was something most attractive about his easy yet laconic manner. He stood up from the foot of the bed on which the little turquoise Buddha still squatted, undisturbed, as men approached along the passage. A policeman on duty outside the door admitted them, and two Chinese police officers came in. Studying their faces, Mannering marvelled at the difference between them and the contrast between them and the two attackers. It was almost incredible that he had thought it hard to tell Chinese individuals apart.

"Did you get them?" Lovelace asked.

"No, sir. They escaped very quickly down a ventilator shaft into Middle Street, and then Peking Road swallowed them up. But we have many fingerprints."

"Not much use until we've nobbled them," remarked Love-

106

lace. "Well, it can't be helped. Do you think you could give us a clear description, Mr. Mason? Not just that they were yellow-faced, slit-eyed, and had distended nostrils?"

Mannering chuckled; he liked this man.

"One of them was as faceless as that but the real villain wasn't, Chief Inspector. Now let me see what I can recall. His right eye was slightly higher than his left and looked slightly smaller, as if it was deformed at birth or else as the result of an operation in childhood—I didn't notice any scar. He had a small mouth, and one corner of his upper lip—the left-hand corner—was ridged, as if he'd once been burned there and the burn had not properly healed. He had a longer face than most of the Chinese I've seen, and his cheek-bones were not so prominent as most of them." He was aware of the policemen as well as Lovelace staring at him in surprise; at least he had managed to shake the detective's nonchalance. When he had finished, Lovelace turned to his men.

"You heard that. Go and get the description circulated at once." As the men turned away, he looked back at Mannering with a smile, and said: "Not F.B.I.?"

"No, sir," Mannering said firmly. "Not now, not any time. Now you can tell me something. Will this get into the newspapers or on the air?"

"In a very nebulous way," Lovelace said. "An apartment at the Peninsular was entered and the occupant robbed—is that all you want?"

"It's certainly everything."

"When do you want to see Sir Hugh?"

"Who did you say?"

"Sir Hugh Brabazon."

"Now I understand you—the Police Commissioner," said Mannering. He should have remembered that Brabazon had been knighted in the last Honours List, but ignorance would probably make him seem even more convincingly American. "What would be a good time? What time do you have right now?" He looked across at his wrist-watch, on the dressing-table.

107

"Just after seven," said Lovelace. "You couldn't have chosen a worse night."

"Why not?"

"The American Consul-General is giving a reception on board the aircraft-carrier in the harbour," Lovelace told him. "As he and Sir Hugh are close friends, Sir Hugh will stay throughout the evening. But as an American citizen you will be welcome to the reception, and I shall be on duty there. If you need any help in presenting that message of introduction, call on me." He gave that rather lazy and attractive smile, and took a small linen bag from his pocket; a manilla envelope was tied to it. "Not that I think you'll need anything but this. Here's your permit to carry a gun, and here's your gun back. We decided that anyone who had taken a chance by helping Li Chen would need something to protect himself with, and it appears we were right."

He turned towards the door, leaving the package on the bed where he had been sitting. Mannering allowed him to reach the door, and then called:

"Lovelace."

Lovelace half turned. "Yes?"

"How serious is the threat to the Li Chens and their shop?"

"It is very serious."

"Can't you put a guard on their premises day and night?"

"We already have a guard," Lovelace told him. "Two men were watching there this afternoon, but they made the mistake of rushing after the man who threw a hand-grenade case at the window, and the real attack came from two men who were on foot. If you want to know more about the situation, talk to Sir Hugh." He nodded, and went out; and this time Mannering did not call him back.

Instead, Mannering leaned back in the chair, staring at the ceiling, and the top of the window against which a red neon sign was flashing. It was dark outside but for the artificial light; night had dropped very quickly. There were the usual noises of traffic, an occasional hoot from a ship at sea, once a shrill train whistle, but he was only half aware of these things. He was warm, snug, and alive; and that was something to be deeply grateful for. He did not know whether the men would have killed him, and he would never know. It was worth assuming that anything else which happened here would be acutely dangerous. The police were highly competent—that was a good thing to know—and yet there remained this danger to the Li Chens, which the police seemed so powerless to prevent. The whole situation was puzzling, even bewildering; and the best chance of learning more about it lay in Sir Hugh Brabazon.

Mannering wondered if he would pass at the American Consulate as an American; that would be the ultimate test.

He got up, cautiously. His shoulders ached, and there was a red-hot pain at the back of his neck where it had been pressed forward by the bath. He massaged it gently and gingerly, inspecting his puffy lips as he did so. He washed them as gently as he could and rubbed in a vanishing-cream-based salve; when he had finished he looked better. He went to his hanging travel robe in the wardrobe; it was empty, but all of his clothes were hanging, one of the room boys had been busy. His suitcase had been unpacked, too.

His heart began to beat faster with a new kind of anxiety. In that case there had been his make-up box, everything he needed to make-up and to cleanse his face and reassume his real identity. He picked the black moroccan-leather case up. It should be locked. He tried the catch, and it opened easily; it had been cleverly and neatly forced. He stood very still as he looked down at it, and then lifted out the top tray, which had most of the paints; underneath was another section containing gum, hair, false eyelashes, cheek pads, even rubber sheaths to work over his teeth to alter their shape and colour. In this compartment he kept his British passport as John Mannering, and his letters of credit.

The letters of credit were gone; so had the passport.

Did that mean that Lovelace had searched and found it? Or had the two assailants taken it before they had come to question him? If they had, then they knew his true identity.

109

14
THE RECEPTION

No doubt it was partly delayed shock from the attack, and partly it was the fault of understanding just how dangerous this made his own predicament. Whatever the reason, Mannering felt a wave of weakness which ran through his body from his knees to his head. He sat down heavily in the nearest chair, with the make-up case in his hands. A tube of flesh-coloured grease-paint, loosened when he had moved the top tray, slipped and fell. He did not attempt to pick it up. After a few minutes he realised that he needed a drink, above everything else; something to stimulate him. He looked pale and felt very shaky as he pressed the service bell. Wraith-like, the room boy appeared. Mannering saw that his right eye was swollen, and his lip cut; yet the man had not said a word of complaint and had behaved as if nothing had happened.

"You require something, sir?"

"A whisky and soda, in a hurry," Mannering said.

"One glass, sir, or a bottle of whisky and some bottles of soda water?"

"I'll have the bottles. Haig."

"Very good, sir." He bowed his way backwards to the door and went out; the door closed with a snap. Mannering, rather better now that he was on his feet again, went to the window and looked out.

He would not have believed it possible that any sight could draw the tension and the weakness out of him, thrusting him into a mood of complete oblivion except the scene before his eyes. Yet the scene which confronted him did exactly that. There were a myriad of lights of every conceivable colour, sharp and clear against the dark water and the dark-blue starlit sky. Every shade, every hue, every contrast stretched out in front of him, and as far as the eyes could see. There were not only the lights in the tall buildings across the water on Hong

110

Kong Island, and the lights in the houses and on the streets of the peak; there were the moving lights on the water, some like giant fireflies, some like moving beacons—lights from the ferries, the junks, the sampans, the warships in the harbour, some of them gaily dressed, in festive mood. He had not seen ships illuminated by coloured lights and floodlights since the victory celebrations after the war. It was not only the beauty of the colouring, it was the speed of the movement everywhere—and most of the moving lights seemed to converge on the largest of the warships, the *Chesapeake,* a carrier of the United States Navy. It looked sombre and grey against the brightness and the beauty of the afternoon scene. He was still watching this, not quite believing it was real, when there was a tap at the door. He turned round.

"Come in."

The room boy was already halfway in, with a tray, ice, Scotch whisky, soda water, and two glasses. Why two? The boy deposited the tray on a table near a luxurious armchair, stood back, and bowed.

"Everything all right, sir?"

"Yes, fine, thanks. What do they call you?" Mannering asked.

"I beg pardon?"

"What's your name?"

"My name, sir, is Wang Lu."

"Did they hurt you much this afternoon?"

"Not very much, sir, only a little. Not so much as they hurt you. I wish to say I am very sorry I allowed it to happen, sir. I was not careful. I hope you will accept my apology, please." He looked both anxious and pathetic as he spoke.

"Wang, you don't have to apologise to me," Mannering said. "I brought it on your head and I'm very sorry about it. Wouldn't you like some time off, so as to take it easy?"

"No, sir, I am perfectly all right, thank you. Is there anything more?"

"Not a thing," said Mannering, but as Wang began a digni-fied kind of shuffle back, he changed his mind. "Oh, yes, there

111

is. Do you happen to know where the American Consul's reception is being held tonight?"

"Of course, sir. Reception is on board big American ship, aircraft-carrier *Chesapeake*. You are to go, sir?"

"Yes."

"I will put out your clothes——"

"It's all right," Mannering said. "I'll do it."

"Please sit down and have drink, sir, and I will put out your clothes. It is all right not to have dinner suit, many air travellers do not have one these days." Wang Lu sounded as if he disapproved of that. "I clean shoes," he announced after spreading out the suit, a clean shirt, a bow tie, and two handkerchiefs. "Reception go on to midnight, there is no hurry."

He went out.

Mannering felt the whisky gradually warming and comforting his body, but it made the back of his head throb even more than before, and he began to wonder whether it had been wise to drink. His headache was very bad indeed when he was dressed except for his shoes. He took three aspirins—Lorna always made sure that he had some in his case—but they did not greatly help. He began to feel impatient for his shoes; Wang Lu was taking a long time.

Five minutes passed, and Mannering began to worry in case something else had gone wrong, but it had not. Wang Lu came back with the shoes shining like .polished ebony; he placed them on the floor at Mannering's feet, stood back, and said:

"I arrange hotel taxi, sir. The launches for the reception leave from special pier near Star Ferry. Taxi take you straight to the pier. Please, you do not forget your passport, it is very important at receptions."

"I won't forget," Mannering said.

Quite suddenly and without the slightest warning, he wondered if there could be any significance in the remark; if Wang Lu was telling him that he had seen the other passport. Had there been a real fight, or simply a pretence at one? Had he let the raiders in? Had he even helped them to search the room? There was no way of being sure, but it was useless for Mannering to try to tell himself that he was hopelessly wrong; he could be right. He must be careful with Wang Lu, with everyone whom he did not know could be trusted.

How could he be sure of anyone except the police?

Wang Lu was waiting at the lift when he left the room, and pressed the call-button the moment he appeared. He bowed as Mannering stepped into the big lift car. The lift-man was big for a Chinese, and had a face not unlike the raider whom he remembered so well. Now he was really getting everything out of focus; all Chinamen *were* beginning to look alike, he wasn't proof against that idea after all.

A large taxi was waiting. Two rickshaw boys, at the end of the driveway, looked at him yearningly, and one called out:

"Rickshaw much better than taxi."

Bumping up and down in that would just about tear his head from his shoulders, Mannering thought wryly. He got into the taxi, and the driver started off smoothly and slowly. He turned right towards the ferries which Mannering had seen from the air but not from the land. The Star Ferry terminal was a blaze of light, and hundreds of people were scurrying towards it and away from it; scurrying was the only word, everyone seemed to be in a hurry. Mannering made himself look round, and saw three sets of headlights not far behind; it was possible that any of the cars was deliberately following him. Was this driver reliable?

They pulled up slowly at a small pier, floodlit and gay with coloured lights, with American sailors in white standing alertly at attention, two or three civilians waiting, twenty or thirty Chinese, including two rickshaw boys, clustering around. Mannering got out.

"How much is that?"

"With the best compliments of the hotel, sir. They are very sorry such a bad thing should happen to you." The little driver smiled and bowed, and skilfully evaded a tip.

Mannering stepped into the blaze of light, and an even brighter light flashed as someone took a photograph. Two sailors and a civilian stepped forward.

113

"A launch is just coming alongside from the *Chesapeake*, sir," the civilian said. "May I have your name please?"

"Sure. I'm James C. Mason." Mannering took the false passport from his pocket and handed it over; the man glanced at it more carefully than he appeared to, and handed it back.

"Glad to have you with us, Mr. Mason. If there's anything you need while you're in Hong Kong, just call on us."

"Why, thank you."

Mannering looked out into the harbour, where so many lights glowed, and the outline of the aircraft-carrier was vivid and gay, as if designed to conceal the menace which the great ship could create.

A launch bedecked with coloured lamps and flags pulled alongside; only the crew was in it. A dozen or so people already waiting went ahead of Mannering. As he stepped forward to the head of the pier, he saw Lovelace hovering on the edge of the crowd, smiling but showing no other sign of recognition. It was a good thing to feel that the police were taking no chances, and——

He felt something clutch his ankle.

On one side the water lapped gently, reflecting the lights and the shadows; just ahead were the others stepping on to the launch—and underneath the wooden pier was a man tugging at his leg, trying to make him lose his balance. Mannering grabbed a wooden post. He nearly lost his balance, and did not realise that as he moved, he crushed the detaining hand against the wooden post. He heard a screech, and felt the grip relax. He saw the hand disappear, and heard a splash. On the instant, searchlights from stationary cars snapped out, vivid and bright, and began to move about the water. Mannering saw the head and shoulders of a man swimming as several sailors, and Lovelace, came running along the wooden pier.

"You all right, sir?"

"You okay?"

"What was it, Mr. Mason?"

Mannering said: "I guess I slipped." That might satisfy the sailors although it certainly wouldn't be good enough for

114

Lovelace. He wanted desperately to go on board the *Chesapeake*, and was afraid that this might stop him; a word from Lovelace most surely could. Then he realised that everything had happened so quickly and those lights had been snapped on; the sailors had undoubtedly been warned to look out for trouble.

Would they stop him from going?

"Are you all right to take this launch, sir? The Admiral's launch will be here in ten minutes and you would be very welcome on board." It was the man who had examined his passport.

"This one, thank you," Mannering said, thankfully. He allowed them to hand him over the side of the pier to the thwarts of a launch where the dozen passengers were now sitting, watching him with curiosity and concern. A sailor steadied him until he was sitting down, and the launch began to move crisply, with the wind fresh and cool against his forehead and face. He was aware of the inquisitive glances of all the other passengers, but kept looking across the harbour towards the lights of the island. Now no one spoke to him. For a second time the fascination of the scene drew fears out of him, making him oblivious of everything else except a kind of suspended anxiety. Almost before he expected it, they were slowing down to go alongside. The *Chesapeake* looked enormous and the lights were less dominating here; the great length and solid hull were awesome. Lights shone on the floating platform fastened to the bottom of the aircraft-carrier's accommodation ladder, lights ran up the side of the ship. Officers in service dress whites were at a middle platform, and the top one which was level with the hangar deck.

Mannering stepped on to the gangway, and he was halfway up the shallow steps of the ladder before he realised that his headache had gone—swept away by the moment of near-panic on the pier. There was another curious fact; he knew what had happened, knew there had been another attempt to kill him by drowning, and that there was no, or little doubt, that he was known to be John Mannering, but—it did not worry him. His

115

hand slid over the varnished wooden rail, and he began to appreciate the spit and polish of the stainless steel and brass-work of the ladder. The officer of the deck stood at the quarter deck, with the bosun's mate just behind him, as if ready to lift the pipe on the lanyard round his neck to pipe the guests on board. He did not; but there were the formalities of "I request permission to come aboard, sir," from the officer with the party and a welcome aboard for each guest.

Grey, seemingly wingless, aircraft, their wings folded while they were on the hangar-deck, had a curious chill gleam. Above Mannering's head were hundreds of gaily coloured flags, ahead of him long tables set with cutlery and glasses, laden with turkeys and hams, a cold buffet to dream about, then the vice-consul and one of the most attractive women he had seen for a long time welcomed him in his assumed name. He was passed on from one to another, offered food and drink, all non-alcoholic, which was just as well if he did not want to bring his headache back. Airmen or seamen, he wasn't sure which, hovered around as the party from the launch moved along the huge deck. Every corner seemed to have its groups of men and women, eating and drinking. Rare and exotic deli-cacies were thrust in front of him in bewildering succession by men in spotless white. On one table there was a cake, a model of the carrier which looked big enough to fill a small room. Music from *South Pacific* seemed to come from a big but unseen orchestra. Most of the airmen and sailors were Euro-peans, but there were some Chinese, some negroes, some Japanese.

Mannering had that curious sense that wherever he moved he was being watched. The guests were as cosmopolitan as any group could be, the dresses as exotic as the food, from saris to long evening gowns, cocktail dresses to burnous. There were diamond tiaras, bejewelled turbans, and magnificent mantillas; it was like a pre-war reception, quite beautiful in every way. Voices were subdued in the corners but grew louder the larger the group. At last Mannering was handed up to a spot beneath a huge *No Smoking* sign. There an Admiral Mannering knew

116

from photographs and the American Consul-General waited to receive them.

The Admiral was brisk, breezy, amiable; two women cornered him. The Consul-General was a tall, rather willowy man with iron-grey hair brushed back from his forehead in waves, immaculate in tails, quiet-voiced, easy-mannered. His wife hardly came up to his shoulder. She was a plump little dove of a woman, homey and homely, dressed in a magnificent sequined gown of sea-green colour. Their escort took the group up, the Consul-General shook hands with them all, and said to Mannering:

"Glad to have you with us, Mr. Mason. And I'm glad you came to no harm this afternoon. If you don't mind mixing business with pleasure, Sir Hugh Brabazon would like a word with you." He rested a hand lightly on Mannering's forearm, then turned to the next guest. A man who had shepherded the party through looked up at Mannering with a bright grin, and said:

"Would you like to meet Sir Hugh now, sir?"

"I certainly would."

"This way, please." He found a path as if by magic through the massed crowd, led Mannering along a wide corridor, and then through a hatch. Once beyond that the festive air disappeared, here was the ship prepared as if for sea, grey, somehow forbidding, the ceiling a mass of pipes and wires. For a wild moment Mannering thought that he was being led into danger from the very heart of safety.

They reached a doorway, and the bright-faced young man tapped, then opened the door and stood aside, saying:

"Mr. Mason, sir."

Sir Hugh Brabazon rose from a chair in a small wardroom, which might have been in any ultra-modern building. He was a short, broad-shouldered, rugged-looking individual, vaguely like a sheep dog, with shaggy eyebrows and grizzled hair which really needed trimming. He was alone, and Mannering could not ask for more.

The door closed.

117

"Now, Mr. Mannering," said the Police Commissioner, "supposing you tell me all about everything." He paused to allow the significance of the "Mr. Mannering" to sink in, and then asked: "But first, what will you have to drink?"

15

MOOD OF AGGRESSION

BRABAZON was obviously very pleased with himself; in fact he was almost smug. It was ridiculous, yet Mannering felt a flare of annoyance with the man, as he might if he had been hoaxed by someone whom he did not like. He hoped that he concealed the hostile reaction as he smiled, sat down on a swivel chair, and asked mildly:

"May I have bitter lemon, by itself?"

The Commissioner looked startled. "Plain? Are you on the wagon?"

"Those with bruises on their cranium shouldn't make the blood run hot," Mannering said.

"Oh, I see. Come to think, your eyes are a bit bloodshot. You're not feeling too bad, are you?"

"Just vengeful," Mannering said. He watched the other man pour out; there was a small table next to the steel desk, with a comprehensive display of drinks on it. "How did you find out?" He took the glass, and sipped. "Cheers. Was it you who took my British passport?"

Again Brabazon looked startled. "No. Lost that, have you?"

"It was stolen this afternoon, and I thought your men might have taken it."

"We didn't, or I would have been told," said the Commissioner confidently. "Was anything else stolen?"

"Some letters of credit, that's all."

"You can make sure you don't lose anything over them,"

118

observed the other bluffly. "And we can do something about the passport if you don't get it back. No, we found out from that Webley .33 of yours. The Yard had warned us that you were likely to pay us a visit and among the odds and ends of information they sent was that you carried a Webley .33 and had a British licence. Your fingerprints were on it."

After a very long pause, Mannering said softly: "Oh, were they?"

Brabazon nodded, and looked at him curiously. A telephone bell rang and he had to turn away to pick up the receiver. Mannering sat very still, playing with the stem of his glass and trying to still his raging temper. Not only had Bristow "warned" the Hong Kong police, when he was here virtually at the Yard's request, but he had sent a set of fingerprints, as he would if any known criminal were going to visit the Crown Colony. Out of the Baron's past there came a whiff of fear, which added fuel to the hot flame of his temper. The Baron's fingerprints had never been taken, but in those days when Bristow had suspected him of being the Baron, his own had been. It was useless telling himself it was a good thing his identity could be proved beyond any doubt; he was livid.

Brabazon was saying: "... Yes, I fully understand.... Yes, in about ten minutes, sir." He paused, then put the receiver down and brushed a hand across his forehead. "The Governor is up top, and wants to talk to me—probably about the Li Chen business. So we'll have to postpone our chat, unless there's something useful you can say in five minutes."

"I can tell you everything I intend to tell you in three," said Mannering. "Presumably you know what Bristow told me and there's no need to repeat that. In India ..." He spoke with a lucidity matched only by its brevity, and Brabazon began to look pensive. After he had described the murder of the beggar woman and his talk with Raymond Li Chen, he went on: "So I came to Hong Kong in the hope that I might be able to help, believing that I was more likely to get by if I posed as an American. You know what's happened here, so I need not go into that again, either." Mannering's voice was like ice. "What

119

you can do is tell Bristow that I'm through with this job, once and for all, and that if he ever sends my fingerprints to another police force on any excuse whatsoever I'll sue him and the Yard for defamation."

Brabazon was staring at him in obvious amazement. Mannering, still feeling as angry as he sounded, got up without another word. There was a tense silence in the room and it seemed to drag on for a long time. Then in a composed but rather subdued way, the Commissioner said:

"Bristow did it for your own good, you know. He told me that you often adopt disguises, and that if we ever needed to prove your identity, all we had to do was to take your prints. If we'd found you dead instead of alive in that bath tub at the Peninsular, we'd have been able to identify you without any trouble at all."

"I find that most reassuring," Mannering said.

Brabazon opened his mouth as if to speak again, then closed it, shrugged, half smiled, and said:

"Well, I mustn't keep the great man waiting. Would you care to meet him?"

"Not in my present mood, thanks."

"Perhaps you're wise," conceded Brabazon, and he smiled more widely. "It may soothe your ruffled feathers a bit to know that you fooled all the Americans you met tonight, although they were taking a special interest in you—they knew what had happened at the Li Chens' shop in Kowloon, although not what happened at the Peninsular. They've a very special interest in the investigation, because so many American nationals have treasures stored at Li Chens'—millions of dollars' worth. A great many bought goods believing they could get a genuine certificate of origin, but could not. Others feel that the money involved is so small compared with the cultural value that the embargo is ridiculous. However, even the vice-consul, who spent seven years in London and knows you by reputation and sight as Mannering, doesn't seem to have had the slightest inkling that you were a limey. Er——" He opened the door. "Sleep on it, will you?" As they stepped outside and a negro rating sprang to attention, he added almost as if against his will: "We could use your help, we're in a damned awkward situation, and—well, as I say, sleep on it."

It would be ungracious to refuse.

"Yes, I will."

"That's good," said Brabazon. "I'll call you in the morning. Let me know if there's anything I can do."

Much mollified, Mannering followed him up to the hangar-deck. This man was not easy to shake, and undoubtedly Mannering had shaken him. When he was on his own for a few minutes, eating fingers of game pie of a quality he did not expect to find outside England, he wondered what had made him blow off like that. Brabazon's manner of half laughing, half deriding him had contributed, no doubt, but there was much more to it. He believed he knew what. He had been pushed around a great deal since this affair had started. In fact practically nothing had been done on his own initiative, and that was not a situation which he liked. By nature he liked to be on the attack, even if it was in defence; yet he had been on the retreat most of the time. He would never forget how much on the defensive he had been when he was so helpless in that bath.

He wanted to strike back, and he had struck at Brabazon.

"That wasn't very clever," he admitted to himself. "And the mood could be dangerous." If he was to be effective in this or in any other investigation, then he had to be detached and not involved; objective, not emotionally angry. Perhaps it was a good thing that he had flown off the handle at Brabazon; it would warn him to be very much more careful. The wise thing now would be to meet the Governor, if only to show Brabazon that he was not sulking.

He moved towards a little group of which Brabazon was one, and then saw Paul Vansitter, one of New York's most prominent fine art dealers, undoubtedly here for the exhibition. It was remarkably easy to forget the exhibition because of the more urgent problems.

Would it be staged?

121

Vansitter, a dapper, sandy-haired man with a Van Dyck beard, saw him but showed no sign of recognition, another fillip to his ego. Brabazon caught sight of him, and a pretty little woman detached herself from the group around the Governor, and approached him, smiling.

"Mr. Mason, I'm Jane Brabazon. My husband would be so glad if you would come and meet the Governor and his wife..."

The Governor, whom Mannering knew slightly and who was a member of one of Mannering's clubs, was elderly, military, amiable to everyone, but there was an expression in his eyes which made Mannering wonder whether he felt quite as well-disposed as he seemed to. His wife, fifteen years or so younger, had a model's distinction, a model's slimness and gracefulness, with a hint of charm in her model-like aloofness. She was utterly uninterested in James C. Mason, but as Mannering moved away he saw her charm melt her aloofness when two Chinese couples came up, the women dressed by some Oriental Dior and with gowns of such colouring it was hard not to stare. The men were very correct in their dress suits and carnations. The Governor's wife appeared thoroughly to enjoy talking to them, and Mannering watched them thaw.

"She's the diplomat of the two," remarked Brabazon. "She can get women as well as men eating out of her hand—you must meet her as John Mannering before you go back, you might find she isn't quite the same. How about a drink?"

"I haven't slept yet," Mannering said drily.

Brabazon, his poise regained and his humour good, grinned lazily at his wife.

"You'll have to work on Mr. Mason, I got on the wrong side of him, Dee. Persuade him that I'm really a reasonable and competent individual, will you? Oh, that reminds me, Mr. Mason—the Governor did want to talk to me about the exhibition which the Li Chens are staging next week. Three different plenipotentiaries have asked him whether it's still on—they've heard rumours that it's been cancelled."

"Has it?"

"No," answered Brabazon. "We're going to make sure that nothing happens at the show, if we can't do that then I might as well hand in my resignation."

"Don't do that, dear," said Dee Brabazon. "I want another winter here before going back to England. Why don't you come and meet..." She seemed to know everybody at the reception, she kept up a running ripple of conversation, and there was a bright, almost mischievous twinkle in her eyes most of the time, as if she knew that her real job was to put her companion into a good humour, and did not mind if she had to be coquettish to succeed.

Then Mannering saw the woman who had been at the shop that afternoon, wearing a high-necked Chinese gown of gold brocade; she looked like a queen. By her side was Charles Li Chen. Talking to another, tiny woman who did not look Chinese but was probably Vietnamese, was Raymond Li Chen. So he had not lost much time flying from Bombay. Paul Vansitter moved across to talk to Raymond. Mannering noticed that Brabazon was near him, then saw Lovelace and the shorter, plumper, darker policeman whom he had seen that afternoon. The truth was that the Li Chen family was under close surveillance—and that could only mean one thing.

Brabazon half expected an attack on them now.

The woman glanced up and saw Mannering. Immediately she moved towards him, saying something to the brothers, who turned with her.

"Mr. Mason, I want to tell you again that we shall never be so grateful," said the woman.

"I am told of the great service you rendered to my brother and to my wife," said Raymond Li Chen. "I am exceedingly grateful also, Mr. Mason." Not by so much as a flicker did he show any sign of recognition. "It was a happy chance that you were in the shop at that particular time. I hope that you will command me and any of my family for any service we can render you—any service at all."

Mannering smiled.

123

"You exaggerate," he said. "I simply pulled a gun and frightened the bandits off. Do you know Lady Brabazon?"

"But of course . . ."

A Chinese rating came up with a tray of smoked salmon on diamonds of brown bread and butter, and some anchovies on fingers of toast. Mannering took one, Lady Brabazon said: "I simply daren't, I'm eating far too much." Mrs. Raymond Li Chen refused almost impatiently, so did her husband, but Charles raised his hand to the tray; he chose anchovy.

Mannering, his senses very alert, noticed two peculiar things. First, as Charles Li Chen stretched out his hand, the rating turned the silver tray at least three inches, so that the natural selection was different from what it would have been had he not done so; and as soon as Charles had the morsel in his hand, the rating turned away. The tray was three-quarters full, but he did not pause to offer it to anyone else. He threaded his way quickly through the crowd. Suspicion flared up in Mannering's mind. He saw Lovelace move forward, speaking sharply to another man in a lounge suit, but Lovelace was too far away to stop Charles from eating the titbit. Mannering was not. He sprang forward, jolted the man's arm, then bent down as if groping for something on the floor. The anchovy and the toast fell only a few inches away from him. He straightened up, as if in embarrassment.

"I'm sorry, I thought I saw an earring on the floor. I'd certainly hate it to be trodden on."

"An earring?" Lady Brabazon's hands rose to her face, and every woman present touched her ears. Another rating came forward and picked up the anchovy and toast, holding it carefully in the palm of his hand. Lovelace beckoned a man with a tray. A young American came up, bright-faced, bright-eyed, to see that all was well. Charles Li Chen had an abundance of titbits thrust in front of him, and seemed to purr with satisfaction as he gobbled.

"I think we ought to go and have a word with my husband," Lady Brabazon said. "Have you had enough chaperoning, Mr. Mason?"

124

"You've been very gracious, very tactful, and highly successful," Mannering declared. "Will you tell Sir Hugh that I'll be glad to talk to him again in the morning, and to do what I can to help."

"I'll be very pleased to," Lady Brabazon said. "Is there anyone else whom you'd like to meet?"

"I don't think so," said Mannering. "I guess I'll pay my respects and go ashore."

The Li Chens were with another group of Americans, Paul Vansitter among them, and Mannering saw Christiansen bearing down. He did not ask himself how the ex-patriot Norwegian had managed to get invited to the reception, but after he had a word with the Consul and his wife, he saw the Hos from London moving forward, towards the group.

It was not until he neared the accommodation ladder that he realised how warm he had been. Dozens of others obviously felt the same and yet were loth to leave; the perimeter of the vast deck was dotted with couples and little groups. Mannering did not linger, but went straight towards the ladder. An officer stood by.

"Thank you, thank you very much," Mannering said.

"Our pleasure, sir," the officer said.

Almost at once, Lovelace appeared, and led Mannering away.

"There's a police launch down there waiting—may I give you a lift?"

"Why, thank you," Mannering said. He walked down the gangway behind the tall detective and stepped into the smaller launch, which in the bright lights looked spick and span and newly painted. No one else seemed to be on board except two Chinese at the controls. The engine roared and they started across the harbour so fast that they seemed certain to ram a big lighted ferry which was crossing the calm water like an enormous floating bus.

"I've never seen anyone move quicker," Lovelace said above the staccato beat of the engine. "I think we would have had a difficult job persuading old Li Chen to cough that lot up, but if he hadn't he would have been in a bad way."

"So it was poisoned?"

"Potently. With arsenic. The anchovy would have hidden the flavour, of course, if you hadn't spotted it he would probably be writhing by now."

"Unless you'd made him cough it up," Mannering said drily. But he felt very tense; if "they" could actually manage to poison their victims on board the aircraft-carrier, what else could they do, and where could anyone be safe? "Did you catch the waiter?"

"Yes," said Lovelace. "He's busy swearing he didn't know anything about it. He said he got a member of the crew from San Francisco to smuggle him on board so that he could get a good tuck-in. I don't know how easy it will be to break him down. Care to come and see us try? He went ashore ten minutes ago."

"I'm quite sure you don't need any help from me," said Mannering. "And believe it or not, I'm tired."

"That's a point. You'd be welcome, but please yourself. I think——" He broke off as they slewed round to go alongside the pier, then stared at several uniformed men lining the quayside, obviously waiting for him, as obviously all very much on edge. In a crumpled heap behind them, with one man on his knees beside it, was a white-clad, crumpled heap. "My God!" breathed Lovelace. "It looks as if he's been killed."

126

16

A CONFERENCE OF EXPERTS

THE white-clad heap was the Chinese who had given the poisoned morsel to Charles Li Chen. The back of his head had been smashed in, and as he saw the blood-pinked water running from his head, Mannering had a mental image of the little beggar woman of Bombay, with just such a wound as this.

Lovelace was talking in a harsh voice and in Chinese; Mannering did not understand a word he said, but knew that he was really letting himself go. A bell clanged and an ambulance drew up, bringing crowds flocking from the ferries and the main street to stare blankly at what was going on.

Lovelace joined Mannering.

"He jumped overboard as the launch touched the pier—the bloody fools hadn't got him handcuffed. No one actually saw the attack, but he must have been killed while in the water. Swim like a fish, some of these chaps. The searchlights showed up his body, and they brought him ashore just before we arrived. I'll have their bloody necks for this." He was bitterly angry, and no doubt felt a sense of both guilt and shame. He could not have ordered the man to be handcuffed—and he was ashamed that this could happen to a prisoner. "Looks as if I'm going to be here for a long time yet. Can I get one of our chaps to drive you back?"

"It's only a step," Mannering said. "I'll walk, thanks."

"The two men standing under that lamp-post will follow you; you needn't be afraid of them," said Lovelace. "We mean to keep some of our witnesses alive."

Mannering said: "I know how you feel. May I make a suggestion?"

"Yes."

"Telephone Bombay," said Mannering. "A woman—a

127

beggar—was murdered there three nights ago, and had the same kind of wound."

Lovelace's expression seemed to ask: "Have you gone mad?"

"She'd brought me a message from Li Chen," Mannering said.

Lovelace actually backed a pace, and then he said: "I'll call Bombay tonight. Thanks."

Mannering walked across the road, at a spot where it opened out into the different carriageways of the Star Ferry bus station, and the two men followed him. Several shops on the other side, near the dock gates, were still open, one of them with its window filled with hideous curios; it was hard to realise that such junk could be sold so readily where there were so many works of art available. He walked slowly along an empty stretch of the road, with one or two closed shops on one side, the railway station on the other. Two rickshaw boys came pounding up, one from each direction.

"You want ride, boss?"

"Show you sights of Hong Kong, boss, night clubs, brothels, any place."

Mannering said: "No, thanks," and went on. They followed him, insistent, strident, pleading, as if they depended entirely on him for their next day's sustenance. There was no certainty that they were not following him because he was Mannering, that they were not hired, as the dead Chinaman had been hired. He saw the two policemen just behind and felt a sense of temporary security; twice in the past few days he had seen how quickly one could die. He shivered as he turned into the crescent-shaped carriageway of the hotel. Many of the windows had lights in them. The doorway was brightly lit, doormen and porters stood as if anxious for something to do. The rickshaw men gave up. Three men opened the doors for him. The big front hall was dimly lit, an orchestra was playing, many of the tables were occupied. Mannering made his way through to the lift. No one followed, but he saw the two policemen in the doorway. The same lift-man whom he had

128

seen earlier was on duty, and he did not need telling which floor Mannering wanted.

Mannering stepped out into the wide corridor.

Different boys were on duty, two of them near the lift, two of them near his bedroom door. He wished he recognised them but he did not. One of them unlocked his door when he was only halfway along the passage, and stood bowing. Mannering turned in, and the man handed him a note. "Thanks." He went inside and closed and bolted the door; he was in that kind of mood. He checked every corner of the room and the bathroom, including the wardrobes and underneath the beds to make sure no one was hiding here. He went to the window, pulled back the heavy curtains, and looked up and down towards each side; no one was lurking on any of the sills, and the danger was only imagined. He closed the window, and then stood very still, watching the scintillating beauty of the harbour. Suddenly he laughed.

"What an incredible place! Lorna simply won't believe it."

He opened the note, a little uneasy, saw that it was on Police Headquarters notepaper and signed by Lovelace; it must have been here for some time.

"*The two men on night duty are our chaps,*" Lovelace had written. "*Sleep well.*"

Mannering put the note on the dressing-table. He had eaten reasonably well at the reception, even though he had missed dinner; there was nothing he wanted unless it was a cup of tea or coffee, preferably tea. He went to the door, and opened it.

"I bring it at once, sir." One of the boys turned away as if he could not carry out the order quickly enough. By the time Mannering had brushed his teeth and got into pyjamas, the tea was on the bedside table, with some wafer-thin ham sandwiches and some biscuits. He looked at the sandwiches thoughtfully, thinking of the arsenic in the anchovy titbits, but remembering that the flavour of ham was not strong enough to conceal any unpleasant taste. These were all right, he needn't be edgy —and yet he was.

129

All the same, he ate them.

When he switched off the light, the glow from the harbour and from neon signs at nearby buildings made the room almost as bright as day; he should have drawn the curtains. He lay trying to make up his mind whether to get up or not, while the events of the crowded day passed through his mind. It was impossible to sleep like this, he would have to get up, have to get up, have to get up....

A sound of knocking pierced the clouds of sleep, a long, long time later. He heard and resented it, but there was nothing he could do to stop it. He half opened his eyes. It was broad daylight—he had dropped off and must have slept for seven hours or more! The knocking continued; it was at the door. He hitched himself up, and looked at his watch; twenty-five minutes to nine was an hour and a half later than he usually slept. He put a hand at the top of the bedclothes, to push them back, and the telephone bell began to ring, a harsh and insistent note. Exasperated, he said aloud: "Why don't you shut up?" But he hitched himself farther up on the pillows and then stretched out for the instrument. As he drew the mouthpiece to his lips he was on the point of saying "Mannering," and did not quite know how he managed to change the name to "Mason". Undoubtedly the "a" had the short sound, as in Mannering.

"So you were just asleep," said Lovelace.

"Oh, it's you, is it? What else did you think I would be?"

"There was always a risk that you might be dead," Lovelace said. "They've been knocking at your door for the past twenty minutes, and when they couldn't get any reply and couldn't get the door open they telephoned me."

"Why were they so anxious to wake me?" demanded Mannering, wide awake now. His exasperation was quite gone; there was a lot to be said for having the police keep so careful a watch on him. Now he realised that he had dreamed of two battered heads, and he shuddered, as if someone had walked over his grave.

"I asked them to," said Lovelace. "The Commissioner's

compliments, and could you possibly join him at a conference at half past nine? We can have a car there for you at a quarter past, and it wouldn't matter a great deal if you were five minutes or so late."

"Considerate of him," said Mannering. "Yes, I'll be glad to see him. How can I be sure that the car is the right one?"

"You'll recognise the driver," Lovelace assured him.

"Thanks. Have there been any developments?"

"Since last night's attempt to poison Charles Li Chen, there is a last-minute panic about opening the exhibition," Lovelace told him. "That's what part of the session will be about. I'll be seeing you." He rang off.

Mannering replaced the receiver slowly, then leaned back on his pillows. He could understand the new doubts, and could not even make up his own mind whether it would be wise to stage the exhibition or not. Most of the exhibits must be in position already, it could not be arranged in twenty-four hours. He wondered whether the Li Chens knew what had so nearly happened to one of the family last night, and then the tapping started afresh at his door.

"Coming!" he called.

In a way that was little short of miraculous, the moment he unbolted the door and they entered, the room boys had boiling hot tea with them. As he drank, they busied themselves about the room, the policemen tidying up, Wang Lu in the bathroom, then collecting Mannering's clothes and hanging them up, next laying out the only other suit he had with him, the striped seersucker. When he stepped out of the bathroom, dressing-gown loose about him, a breakfast tray was brought in with bacon, eggs, and coffee, all piping hot, marmalade and butter and even croissants which might have been made in any French country kitchen. At twelve minutes past nine he was escorted to the lift, and at nine-fifteen exactly he stepped into a car driven by a young Englishman who had been at the party.

"I'm Detective Sergeant Dowl, sir. Thank you for being so prompt."

131

"Don't thank me; thank the best gentleman's gentleman in the world."

The young man laughed. "They're pretty good, aren't they?" He started off, slid into thick traffic, and drove as if he was part of the mechanism of the car. "These meetings usually take place on the island, but this morning it's at one of the administration buildings near the car ferry."

Mannering succumbed to the fascination of the colourful decoration of the shops and the houses, and the milling masses of Chinese; a European seemed out of place except near the main shopping and tourist districts. Ten minutes' drive took them along a narrow street and then into an open square surrounded by modern buildings, none very tall. The Union Jack flew over all of the buildings, and two or three British soldiers in khaki were on guard duty. The sun was already high and warm, Mannering could have revelled in it had he been on board the *Orienta*.

As a uniformed policeman came from one of the buildings and opened the door for Mannering young Dowl said: "I expect they'll take you back, sir," and drove off. Mannering, unescorted, went into the building, and was met by Lovelace coming down a wide stone staircase.

"We saw you arrive," he explained. "Imagine adding punctuality to all the other virtues!"

"Before we go wherever we're going, who am I likely to meet, and what is the general feeling?"

"You'll probably be Mannering," answered Lovelace. "Sir Hugh is in the chair, and our Assistant Commissioner is there, with the Chief Security Officer for the Combined Armed Forces—oh, and the American Consul-General and one or two other Americans—F.B.I., I shouldn't wonder. So there are some here!" He laughed on a low-pitched note as they reached some double doors guarded by a Chinese in police uniform. "Here we are."

The Chinaman opened the doors. Mannering stepped into a long, rather narrow conference room, which was bright in the morning sun. It was a contemporary room, with pale-brown

132

highly polished wooden-panelled walls, a long, narrow table of the same highly-polished wood, and a picture of the Queen and the Duke of Edinburgh on the wall above Sir Hugh Brabazon. He was sitting in the middle of the far side of the table, flanked by a man whom Mannering had seen at the reception, and the American Consul-General, who looked rather tired, but his highly sensitive-looking face seemed very alert. Two men sitting opposite these were obviously the Americans; each of them swivelled round to see him. Brabazon stood up, welcomed him with a wave of the hand, waited until he was sitting halfway between the two groups, and then introduced him as Mannering to the three Americans; the one name which registered was that of Dooley, the Consul. The man on the Commissioner's right was the Assistant Commissioner; Mannering didn't catch his name.

". . . and we're all grateful to you for coming," said Brabazon, as if he meant it. "We are on what can truly be called the horns of a dilemma, and we don't think that any official personage can help us out of it. There are representatives of both the Chinese governments in Hong Kong, and one of them could possibly be responsible for what's happening over the Li Chen affair. If we make any official representations we'll run into trouble, and anyhow each side will flatly deny it. What we want you to do—not as our representative but as a man highly respected in the antique business all over the world—is to try to find out what they will settle for. That means, what they really want. And you as an individual can really let your hair down," added Brabazon, speaking as casually as if this were the most ordinary request imaginable. "You can accuse each of them of employing gangsters, say, and let us know their reaction. It's really as simple as that."

17

AS SIMPLE AS THAT

"So it's as simple as that," Mannering said heavily.

No one responded, but everyone stared at him, the Americans with even greater intentness than the English. It would be easy to ask: "Why me?" but the question would lead nowhere. He could be sure of one thing: unless they believed that he had a chance of finding out what they needed to know, they wouldn't approach him. For some reason he was regarded as the most likely man to get those results.

At last, Brabazon said: "There shouldn't be any physical danger we can't prevent, now we know the odds. Not in Hong Kong. And if we can find a way of putting an end to this business, there won't be any danger afterwards. I've no doubt that a great deal of trade will result if we do allow the exhibition to open, and you will get your share, so there could be strong business incentives for helping us." He frowned as he saw Mannering's expression, hesitated, opened his mouth wide, and then said: "All right, I withdraw that."

Mannering said drily: "I've no objection to making money, but if I were to make myself a millionaire overnight it wouldn't help if I was found next day with my head looking like the head of the man who was pulled out of the harbour last night. Or the Indian woman, who——"

"Lovelace told us about that, and I've talked to the Bombay police this morning," interrupted Brabazon. "They're being as helpful as they can but it wasn't one of the most important of murders, you know. One of the things which a lot of police would prefer to pretend had never happened. I have to admit that there's a risk. What would tempt you to have a go at this, Mannering? You could perform a great service to your country, or at least this Crown Colony. You have some idea of the tightrope we're walking. And you know how Peking and Formosa love to get at each other's throats. One of these days something could happen which would make Peking decide that we've outlived our usefulness as their back door to the world's trade, and——"

"Do you seriously suggest that this could precipitate that kind of crisis?" demanded Mannering.

"I don't seriously suggest, I say flatly that if this thing goes sour on us any more, it could be disastrous. Look what's happened already. In view of the United States' attitude towards Peking, if there's even a suspicion that a Chinese spy bought his way on board the *Chesapeake* last night and actually attempted to poison a guest at the reception——" Brabazon broke off, looking across at the American Consul-General as if appealing for help.

Dooley said: "Mr. Mannering, we're talking confidentially here, I'm sure you understand that. And confidentially, I can tell you that if this story were to leak into any of our newspapers it could become a very great sensation, possibly the spark to set off a lot of dangerous fireworks. That never helps. If it happened at the wrong time it could cause a shift in emphasis which could disturb the present uneasy truce between us and Peking. I hope you will accept Sir Hugh's assurance that this is a very grave issue indeed." He smiled faintly, and went on: "Now if I were addressing Mr. James C. Mason I would appeal to him as a patriotic American, but I can't hope to influence Mr. John Mannering in that way."

Mannering smiled, very thoughtfully.

"What's on your mind?" demanded Brabazon.

"Heavy doubt as to whether I could be any good at all," replied Mannering.

"Oh, but you could. What we would like you to do is go first to the Peking government's representative—they have a Consul here of course—and tell him what's happened to you. Perhaps tell him you have been told that this is the work of his agents, and——"

"Have him throw me out," said Mannering.

"I wish he would," said Brabazon, warmly. "Then we'd know that he had an outsize in guilty consciences. No,

135

whatever else they'll be polite." He paused, and rubbed both of his big, very white hands together for what seemed a long time, staring into Mannering's eyes all the time. Then he went on with great precision: "We can't make you go. We can only tell you that we have been trying to heal this breach for weeks, and have failed. I admit you are a forlorn hope, but we know you as a man of great integrity and of great ingenuity. We would very much like you to try."

Slowly, Mannering responded: "You want me to see the Consuls of both Chinese governments, tell them what you suspect without letting them know that you suspect it, and ask them if there are any conditions on which they will do a deal?"

Brabazon's eyes lit up. "That's it, in a nutshell!"

"That's it exactly," said Dooley.

"What kind of deal do you envisage?"

"That will probably have to come from them," said Brabazon. His lips curved as if he were trying to stifle sudden laughter. "Or from anyone who happens to have an idea. The whole point of this, John, is that it is an unofficial approach. There must be a way of finding out who is causing all the trouble, and if they are then this should help. It's possible that agents of each or one of the governments is doing it without his government's knowledge, of course—we might be able to get a clue to that, too. *Will* you have a go?"

"What about the exhibition?" asked Mannering. "Is that on or off?"

"Oh, on," said Brabazon without hesitation. "There's a limit to how much face the Li Chens will lose, and in any case everything is now ready—all that's needed is a final polishing up of all the exhibits, and that's being done now. The only possible cause for cancelling the opening would be if a raid on it was likely. We can only say we think there possibly might be but that no one is going to kill the goose of the golden eggs, if you see what I mean. We have a strong guard over the galleries day and night, and no one is allowed in without the Li Chens' written authority. The value, either in hard cash or

136

in foreign exchange or what-have-you is in the actual *objets d'art*, of course. Someone might destroy one or two as a token, or even smash up the contents of one shop, but the hard core of the valuables should be safe enough—that's what they want to get their hands on."

"Safe except for one thing," said Mannering mildly.

"Eh?"

The American Consul-General leaned forward.

"What one thing?" demanded Brabazon.

"If the Peking government think the Formosa government will get the best of this affair they might destroy them simply to make sure that can't come about. And *vice versa*. You could call it a kind of scorched earth policy. It's certainly a risk we ought to take into account."

Brabazon was breathing very hard; Dooley was smiling, but there was a bleakness about his expression.

"You see what we mean," Brabazon said, gustily. "What is needed in this is a fresh mind. You're right of course, but it hadn't occurred to us. We've taken extreme security precautions and now we'll double them, we——" He broke off, with his half-scowling stare, as if he read the answer in Mannering's expression and was prepared to argue about it. "What's on your mind now?"

"A different kind of approach," Mannering answered. "One you could do as well as I could, and probably much better, but I would try if that is how you prefer it." He waited, less to keep them on tenterhooks than to put his own thoughts in lucid order; the notion had come to him quite without warning, and he had not yet had a chance to see its disadvantages. "Supposing each government was asked to assist in the security arrangements at the exhibition? That would be a tacit admission that each has some rights, it might lead the way to some kind of agreement—some way out of the dilemma. And even if I were to make the suggestion," Mannering added drily, "I don't think either side would want to throw me out."

When he finished, Dooley was smiling broadly, as if nothing could have pleased him more. His rather prominent mouth and

137

high cheek-bones made him look not unlike a Red Indian. Brabazon sat with the heels of his hands beating against his forehead, as if this were more than he could stand. Lovelace kept nodding, very slowly and deliberately. The others round the table watched Mannering as if they were hypnotised. No one spoke for several seconds, and the silence seemed to be almost profound.

"Well, now I know one thing," Brabazon burst out. "When Scotland Yard tells me I can rely on a man, I can rely on him." He looked almost shamefacedly at Dooley. "Believe it or not, I nearly stopped Mannering from joining us in this matter."

"I have a feeling that he might have been more difficult to stop than you think," said Dooley drily. "Will you make the approach to both parties, Mr. Mannering?"

"If that's what you would like," Mannering said. "I wouldn't take it for granted that it will come off, but I'm sure it's worth trying."

The Englishman sitting on Brabazon's right, who had not said a word but looked rather solemnly, perhaps worriedly about him all the time, leaned back in his chair as if he were at last able to relax. He was middle-aged, fresh-faced, and had very clear blue eyes.

"Now I'm beginning to think I can report back that it's a fair risk," he remarked. "Why didn't someone think of this before?"

"Chiefly because it wouldn't occur to anyone in our situation that either side would think of joining in," Brabazon said. "That's one of the troubles when we're stuck out here in an outpost, so to speak, all so damned conscious of the delicacy of the position that we look at everything too closely, never see the whole picture. Well, if you're satisfied, Jim, I am."

There was a murmur of agreement round the table. Mannering felt a natural glow of satisfaction, and at the same time a measure of disquiet; if this failed they would be back where they had started, and he did not think there would be time to find another way out of the impasse. He was watching the man with the very clear blue eyes, whose opinion had obviously carried a lot of weight. He wondered if this were Brabazon's Assistant Commissioner, and asked with a chuckle in his voice:

"Does anyone mind telling me who Jim is? I think I've been able to place all the rest of you."

"Didn't you know?" Brabazon could be too ingenuous to be true. "Jim Finnigan represents the combined insurance companies in the Colony. They've a lot at stake in this one way and another—in fact they were all for postponing the exhibition or cancelling it altogether, and Jim wasn't too happy when we decided that we couldn't recommend that. Some of the insurance was taken out by American owners, some by the Li Chens. Every item insured is covered individually, of course."

"How much is insured?"

"Seventy-five per cent of it," Finnigan said. "I know one thing—it'll never be renewed."

"Now, gentlemen, how about some coffee?" Brabazon asked. "Or would any of you care for something stronger?"

It was nearly eleven o'clock. Mannering settled for coffee, several of the others decided to go back to their own offices. Dooley asked Mannering if he could give him a lift back to the hotel. It was a quarter to twelve when the Consul-General dropped him, got out of the car to shake hands and say good-bye, and:

"I must admit I wish that you really could claim American citizenship, Mr. Mason. Thank you again."

Mannering said: "I've a nasty feeling that we're counting our chickens too soon." He watched the big blue Cadillac move off, then turned round. Christiansen was standing by the foot of the big staircase, talking to Vansitter, who seemed always to be pulling at his beard. Mannering approached them and both looked towards him. Had he been his real self, recognition would have been instantaneous; now, neither of them gave him a second look, although he walked straight past them. Vansitter was saying:

"Shall we have a drink?"

139

"And why not?" asked Christiansen. They sat down, and Mannering sat behind them, so placed that he could hear all they said. The most likely subject was shop, and after they had ordered drinks, Vansitter said: "It's a remarkable thing, but it doesn't look as if anyone else is coming. I should not think the Li Chens are very pleased with that."

"In their position I would be most offended," said Christiansen. He had a formal way of talking and his English, although word perfect, was uttered almost as if it were coming from mechanical lips. "I wish I had not changed my mind, but Mannering himself told me that he would be here. In fact . . ."

Mannering did not wait long enough to hear what he said next, but the little he had heard made him very thoughtful indeed. The two Hos from London; Christiansen and Vansitter—it was incredibly meagre a response to a widespread invitation, and virtually an affront to the Chinese hosts. He had an odd feeling; that he wished he could go back to the couple as Mannering, and exchange opinions and ideas, but it was impossible for the time being. He took the lift from this first floor, with two elderly American women who had just come out of a shop called the *Star of Siam* carrying silk dresses over their arms, as excited as if they were buying their first expensive dress.

". . . and back home this real Thai silk will be the envy of everyone . . ."

"And it's so cheap, compared with prices in London or Paris, and as for New York, it's a quarter of the price."

They got out at the fifth floor.

Mannering walked along to his own room. Wang Lu was not in sight until he drew near, when the room boy came at a double shuffle, half smiling. He unlocked the door and stood aside. His eye was bruised but it did not look so angry, and the cut on his lip was almost healed. One of Lovelace's policemen, in the white dress of a houseboy, stood watching from the passage. Mannering closed the door behind him, did not lock it, but looked about him intently. He would not really feel safe until this affair was over.

140

There was nothing to suggest that anyone but the servants had been here.

Mannering went into the bathroom. The bath was half filled with water, reminding him vividly of what had happened here yesterday afternoon. Involuntarily, he shuddered. He had been close to death, but he did know how prodigal these people were with life. A little woman in Bombay, a little man in Hong Kong—who else had died? Who else would die?

He stood looking at the harbour and the unceasing flow of traffic, at the subdued, almost autumnal colouring of the hills of the island beyond, fading into the distance as if it were actually drifting into the sea. The fascination remained; it was almost as if the scene had a mesmeric effect on him, and he started when there was a tap at the door, and Wang Lu said:

"There is gentleman to see you, Mr. Mason."

Mannering turned round as Raymond Li Chen came into the room.

Dressed in a pale-grey, beautifully cut lounge suit, with a single pearl tie-pin in his off-white tie, his hair greying at the temples, Raymond Li Chen was as distinguished now as he had been in full evening dress at the reception. The skin about his hazel eyes was a little puffy, as if he never got enough sleep, but their gaze was very direct. He shook hands as the door closed, glanced out of the window, hesitated, and then turned to face Mannering almost as if he had something unpleasant to say.

"My friend," he said, "I do not think that any of my family can ever be out of your debt. Here in Hong Kong we have many friends, and those who work for us have many friends, also, and so we hear a great deal of what goes on, even though word of it does not appear in the newspapers or over the radio. So we know what nearly happened to my brother last night. We are all shocked that it could have occurred on board an American ship, but even more shocked by what could have happened had you not been so observant and so prompt. We believed that we were in your debt before, but it was nothing to this. I am almost ashamed to ask more help from you, and yet

141

it could be of such great importance. Will you forgive me?"

It was as flowery as it was long-winded, and yet it seemed to come from the heart. Mannering motioned to a chair, waved a disclaimer, and said:

"Of course, I will help if I can."

"I understand you have been to a conference with the police and with other officials," Raymond Li Chen said. "Do you know if they have been able to recommend any specific action?" He paused, and then went on as if he had now really reached the point of all he had come to say: "Do you know if they consider it safe to open the exhibition? I am very much afraid, for fear there should be more attacks of vandalism, such as there was at the shop."

Mannering paused long enough to make it seem that he was giving this deep consideration before saying:

"They think it's safe to open the exhibition, although they didn't tell me what they proposed to do, except that they would redouble the security measures near the gallery. It's a matter of honour that nothing should go wrong, and that the exhibition should be staged."

"I suppose that is something I should be thankful for," said Raymond Li Chen, but he did not look as if he were particularly cheered. "Mr. Mannering, it is not a question of making sure that nothing will go wrong, it is a question of trying to make sure that something will go right. I had thirty-four acceptances to this exhibition. I will make no secret of it to you. I hoped that it would be possible to arrange for some of the dealers to take many of these goods off my hands, I am deeply worried by the fact that I have so much in my stores. Thirty-four acceptances," he repeated, "from dealers in the main European countries, in the United States, in Canada, Australia, the Middle East—but now only a handful of them will come. The others were sent a cable, yesterday, from Hong Kong, saying that it had been cancelled. I have had cables back already, saying that some of the dealers hope that it is only postponed. Is it worth opening the exhibition with so few interested persons present?"

142

18

THE GENERAL

MANNERING seemed to hear Vansitter and Christiansen talking about the poor response; at least they would now be satisfied that the Li Chens would not regard it as an affront. For a few seconds there was nothing he felt he could usefully say, and words for the sake of them had never appealed to him. Very gradually, the expression in Raymond Li Chen's eyes changed, there was positively a spark of humour in them.

"But of course, you are thinking that as you have come so far, then at least you should have the opportunity of seeing the treasures! And there are several dealers here, in all I believe nine arrived before the cables reached them, those who had some other business here, or who decided that Hong Kong in February is the perfect place for a holiday. Mr. Mannering, allow me to ask one more question, and that is the last."

"Yes, of course."

"When you left the conference did you feel that it would be folly for me to open the exhibition?"

"No," answered Mannering promptly. "On the contrary, everyone there seemed to think that the security measures were so good that the risk was a reasonable one. They don't have the last word, of course, you do. They considered asking you not to open the exhibition, and decided not to."

"Then I am very much happier," said Raymond Li Chen. "So will many people be—it is a great occasion for Hong Kong, where there are perhaps more dealers in fine art and *objets d'art* than anywhere else in the world, including the great cities. It has long been my dream to make Hong Kong the true trading centre of oriental antiques, to make it far more, far greater than an enormous bazaar where tourists come and buy a few trinkets or a cheap carving, and go away believing they have a great bargain. As indeed some of them have, but . . ."

143

Raymond Li Chen talked almost dreamily for a long time, and Mannering let him go on, although he was becoming anxious to talk to the two consuls. Abruptly, Li Chen broke off, actually laughed, and said: "But I am becoming garrulous! Everything will go on as arranged, then. Tomorrow, at six o'clock in the evening, we shall open the exhibition with a reception almost as distinguished as that on board the aircraft-carrier. Allow me to show you the gallery where it will be held." He drew Mannering to the window and pointed across the harbour. "First, you see the tall, narrow building, with the red sign on top ... now you look towards your left, past the new ferry terminal, and you see the old building with the flags.... Yes? ... Now look up the hill, towards the top. You see almost immediately above the old building there is a long white one, with no other buildings close to it but with some trees and shrubs.... Yes?"

"I can see it," Mannering said.

"That is the gallery, in the centre of the Ho Sun Gardens. Ho Sun was a wealthy Chinese citizen of Hong Kong who surrounded himself with such treasures as those we shall see there tomorrow. He bequeathed the house and gardens to the Colony, in gratitude for the fact that they allowed him to take up British citizenship when he was a refugee from China in the days of the Boxer Rebellion. It is a museum but is let from time to time for private exhibitions. The one which I have arranged is the most magnificent of them all. I really believe," Raymond Li Chen added, and now he was smiling gently again, "that I would think it worth opening the exhibition if you were the only visitor. Now, I must go. Thank you, thank you a thousand thousand times."

His handclasp was so strong that it was almost painful.

*   *   *

Mannering waited long enough to see his visitor to the lift, before he sat on the side of the bed and put in a call to the Chinese Consulate. On the note that Brabazon had given him

144

there was a name: General Suno. He asked for Suno, and was put through almost at once.

"Ah yes, Mr. Mannering, I will be glad to see you," the General said in excellent English. "What time would be most convenient for you, please?"

"Is half past two all right?"

"It is very suitable," said the General. "I look forward to seeing you very much."

Mannering put down the receiver thoughtfully. The way had been smoothed very quickly, and he began to wonder if there was more in it than met the eye—whether Brabazon was not being even more tortuous-minded than Mannering had considered. He was acutely aware of the strangeness of the circumstances, the differences in the attitudes and the thinking of the Chinese; Europeans who had lived here for some time and had to work closely with them day in, day out, might begain to think in the same way. It was possible that he was being used as a pawn in a game that all of them were playing with consummate skill. As he thought that he pictured Dooley's face, and told himself that the American Consul-General had been completely frank. He wasn't so sure about Brabazon.

He called the second number, the Nationalist government's Consul; here he was to ask for Dr. Hueng Hanno. Again he was put through at once, as if his call had been expected. Dr. Hanno had a very soft, persuasive kind of voice.

"Yes indeed, Mr. Mannering, it will be my privilege to meet you. I have had the pleasure of visiting your famous shop in London, but unfortunately at the time you were not in England. We have mutual interest in fine art, you understand. At what time would it be convenient for you to come and see me?"

"Is half past four suitable for you?"

"It is indeed. I look forward to it very much. For now, Mr. Mannering, *au revoir*."

Mannering put down the receiver this time and stood looking at it. The doubts that he had felt after talking to General Suno were much stronger. Brabazon had been able to say *open*

145

sesame, and all doors had opened. He went to the window and looked across the harbour at the white building, and reflected that it should be easy to guard the place; judging from this distance there were no trees or bushes within fifty yards of the building itself, and nowhere to hide.

It was now half past twelve, and he had not too much time. He telephoned Lovelace, who said:

"If you'll bring your box of tricks along here I'll give you a room in which you can change back to Mannering, and then have you taken to the General. You can decide what to do about James C. Mason when you've finished with the two consuls." Lovelace was brisk and to the point. "There won't be much time for lunch. Shall I fix something for you while you're changing?"

"Please," said Mannering. "I'll get a cab right away."

"There's a car waiting for you outside," said Lovelace.

*   *   *

At ten minutes past two, Mannering stood up from a dressing-table in a small dressing-room set aside usually, he understood, for V.I.P. visitors to the Police Headquarters. As he saw his reflection, he gave a snort of a laugh. Even to him, the change was astonishing, and he had watched himself gradually rub James C. Mason away, and bring back himself. In a peculiar way it was almost as if this face, the face of the cavalier in the office at Quinns, was really the disguise. He had come to Hong Kong as Mason, and in a way he thought that he was thinking as Mason.

He fastened his case, locked it, left it in a corner, and then went outside. A different orderly from the one who had seen him come in was on duty, and so showed no surprise at all. He was led downstairs to Lovelace's office, and went into the small, almost barely-furnished room. Lovelace was on the telephone. He squinted round at Mannering as he was speaking, then suddenly stuttered, turned round, stared wide-eyed, and breathed into the telephone:

"I'll call you back, something's cropped up." He put the

eceiver down slowly, still staring, and said as if fervently: "Thank God you're not a crook! That disguise was masterly." He gave a jerky little laugh. "It would shake a few people, such as the Li Chens, I fancy." He glanced at his wrist-watch and then jumped up. "But you're tight for time. I'll take you down to the car." As they walked down a flight of narrow steps, Lovelace was still talking. "The General is a bit big for his boots, and can be an obstructionist, but at least he always listens and he can make up his mind quickly. Dr. Hanno likes to sleep on all his decisions, but he's generally speaking more progressive and outward-looking than most of the Chinese in Hong Kong."

"Are there any taboos?"

"Meaning?"

"Can I mention the Nationalists to the one and the Reds to the other?"

Lovelace laughed. "Oh, they each know the other exists! All you've got to do is make sure that you don't appear to favour one or the other. Tell me something, Mr. Mannering."

"Yes?"

"Have you decided what your approach is going to be?"

"I haven't decided a thing," Mannering said, "except that there are millions of pounds' worth of some of the most beautiful works of art in the world here in Hong Kong, most of them never seen in the West, and I'd hate to see them destroyed."

"Pious thought," said Lovelace.

At half past two exactly the black Austin car in which Mannering was driven to the Consulate of the Peking government pulled up outside the gateway. Two guards were outside the gates, two armed guards just inside the gates. One came forward to look at the credentials, peered at Mannering much more intently than most immigration officers, and waved the car through. They pulled up outside a large, old-fashioned building, more European than Chinese, and a man in a black coat and striped trousers came hurrying down to open the door and to welcome Mannering. This V.I.P. treatment was puzzling, but he was here and he wanted to go through with it. The

147

General's faculty for making up his mind quickly was the factor on which to pin his hopes.

He was handed on from one secretary to a second, then to a third, then into a long, narrow room, overlooking the harbour. It was so beautifully furnished in traditional Chinese style, except for a high table in one corner, that Mannering almost held his breath.

The General rose from his chair behind the table. He was a short, very broad man, in a beautifully fitted dark-grey suit. On the wall above him was a photograph of Chou En Lai and another of the Chinese President. His face was very round, very brown, smooth shaven except for a wispy moustache which was out of keeping with everything else about him. He had very little hair, and what there was was cut very short; it looked like fluff. As he shook hands with Mannering, a door opened and another man in black coat and striped trousers brought in green tea, in the now familiar little cups without handles.

General Suno might be obstructionist, Mannering reflected, but at least he went straight to the point.

"I am told, Mr. Mannering, that you have some proposals regarding the safe custody and the future of the treasures which belong to China, and which are now in possession of the family of Li Chen. Please understand, I know that there is some argument about the legality of the ownership of the treasures, but my government has no doubt that they were removed from China unlawfully, and like all stolen goods should be returned to their lawful owners. It is regrettable that some individuals should suffer heavy loss in consequence, but——" He shrugged. It was almost possible to believe that he added under his breath: "But as these are mostly Americans, why should we worry?"

"May I be very frank, General?" asked Mannering mildly.

"I am sure that you will be, and I would be disappointed if you were not, Mr. Mannering. It is a common misconception that we Chinese are a cunning and tortuous-minded race. I assure you there is nothing we like better than simplicity,

148

nothing we respect more than truth and integrity of purpose—once we are satisfied of their genuineness. Please—what are your proposals?"

"May I ask one or two questions first?" countered Mannering. "That would make sure that we start from the same point when considering any proposals."

"I will answer if I can."

"Do you agree that the treasures in the forthcoming exhibition are of rare and in many cases unique value?"

"Yes, sir, I do."

"Do you agree that apart from the issue of legal ownership, if they were to be damaged in any way it would be a tragic loss to the world's artistic culture, and particularly to classical Chinese culture?"

"Mr. Mannering," said the General gravely, "I believe it would be an irreplaceable loss. I should perhaps add that in the view of my government these very remarkable objects should never have left the country—they are part of the heritage of our history, and they should be housed in Peking, where one of the old imperial palaces has been set aside for their display."

"Do you think every possible effort should be made to make sure that they are not damaged or destroyed?"

"Yes, most emphatically I do. I am sure that the authorities here, with the most competent police force, will make sure that no act of vandalism can take place."

"General, some very strange things have happened in Hong Kong," said Mannering. "You may or may not know of the attempt to destroy some valuable and historical treasures only yesterday. You may or may not know that last evening it was possible for a Chinese whose identity is not known to secrete himself on board the aircraft-carrier *Chesapeake,* and to attempt to poison one of the guests. My police friends do a very fine job here in Hong Kong, but it is impossible for them to make sure that no one smuggles themselves into some part of the island. You know how many come across the border of the New Territories, and how many come from Formosa by

149

sea. You know better than we can ever do the methods which criminals from either place might adopt to rob or to damage or to destroy. Will you help to guard the collection—inside the Ho Sun Gallery, and in the grounds?"

Throughout all this, the General kept an absolute poker face; it was as if he had suddenly been turned to weathered oak or teak; his eyes did not move, no muscle of his face moved. Mannering had no idea whether he had known about the poisoning or the attack on the Li Chens' shop, and had no idea what kind of reaction he would get from this man. As the seconds passed, he began to fear that it would be antagonistic, if not hostile.

The General asked quietly: "Is Sir Hugh Brabazon aware of the nature of your proposals?"

"Yes."

"Will he accept help from us?"

"Yes."

"Will he also expect help from another place?"

He meant Chiang Kai Shek's government, of course; this was probably the rock on which the proposals would break.

The General pushed his chair back, and moved to the window. He studied the busy harbour and the sunlight shining on the pale mist of the hills and the foreshore for a long, long time. He stood with his hands behind him, the fingers interlocked, and as far as Mannering could judge he did not move a muscle until he turned round.

"Yes," he said. "And I will be happy to discuss details with Sir Hugh at any time convenient to him."

19

THE FORCES OF SECURITY

"MR. MANNERING," said Dr. Hueng Hanno, "will you please allow me a little time to consider these suggestions?—most interesting suggestions, indeed. I might say almost bold. It is most refreshing to meet a person of such directness and such obvious goodwill. May I telephone you at your hotel, shall we say at——" Mannering held his breath, half fearful that Hanno would want too long to consider. "... seven o'clock this evening? That will allow me time to consult my superiors."

He smiled as he spoke, so gently.

The room was large, and even in daylight it had been gloomy because of trees which grew close to two long windows. There was a faint scent of incense on the air, and stillness everywhere. Had he been ushered into the presence of a mandarin in the China of an earlier era, he might have seen a man like Dr. Hueng Hanno, a tall and gracious old man with grey hair and a silky grey beard, a magnificently embroidered mandarin's costume, worn as if he knew no other. About the room were pieces of furniture which would not have been right in a museum, they had an old-worldliness and a shabbiness which suggested that they were part of this man's home, a beloved and precious place which may well have been in his family for generations. Everything was slightly shabby, even the sleeves of the gown were worn.

"Do you mind telephoning me at police headquarters—in Sir Hugh Brabazon's office?"

The doctor said softly: "So this is indeed an official request, Mr. Mannering." He looked as old as time, as wrinkled as cracked parchment, as tough as the ages. No doubt out of courtesy to his visitor he sat at a small table on an upright chair, but lacquer stools and silken cushions dotted about the room were more fitting for him.

151

"There's nothing official about it at all," answered Mannering. "But unofficially I have Sir Hugh's assurance that if he is offered help in security, he will be glad to accept it."

"So he is indeed worried."

"I think he is very anxious that nothing should go wrong with the collection," Mannering said.

"You will tell him, please, that there is no doubt that the collection belongs to the true government of China, what you call the Nationalist government, and that as its representative I must ask for the return of these very valuable things to their rightful owners."

"I'll tell him," Mannering said formally.

"And now, Mr. Mannering, I must give this my most earnest consideration." The doctor's hands appeared from the long sleeves of the gown, and he clapped them gently; he had long, beautifully rounded nails. Almost at once a servant appeared, dressed in the same kind of clothes but without the elaborate embroidery. "Please be assured of my gratitude for the trouble you have taken."

He bowed.

Mannering inclined his head, and followed the servant out of the house and to the waiting car. It was still broad daylight; he had been with the doctor less than half an hour, and preconceived notions that the Chinese were long-winded and irresolute went completely by the board. He suspected that Hanno had already made up his mind what his answer would be, and feared that it would be "no". He wondered if he had given any hint that Peking's representatives had said "yes"; that in itself could be enough to make the Nationalists say "no".

At a quarter to six he telephoned Brabazon and arranged to be at his office at a quarter to seven. He went to the Peninsular Hotel, and booked a room as Mannering. While he was at the desk he looked to see if there were any messages for Mason, but saw none. He registered, said that his baggage would follow, and went along to the telephones and called the letters office.

"No, sir, there are no messages for you," answered the soft-voiced clerk. "Yes, sir, I will inform your floor manager that you require your room but you may not be back tonight ... thank you, sir."

Mannering went into the big lounge, but saw no sign of the other dealers; the very time when he would have been glad to talk to them, they weren't here. He was followed at a discreet distance by Lovelace's men, and that very fact gave him an uneasy kind of feeling; that every step he took might be nearer some unsuspected form of danger. He shrugged that feeling off, and went by foot towards the main shopping district of Kowloon. If all went well he would cross the harbour tonight, he hadn't been on Hong Kong Island yet. Few people were about near the hotel, but the shopping streets were crowded, and he knew that the shops would be open until late, some of them until after midnight, all of them while they thought there might be some business, no matter how small. At every curio shop he paused, marvelling at the old ivory statuettes of emperors and queens, of fishermen and of women drawing water, of ox carts and of snakes. Hong Kong had been the storehouse of ivory and jade carvings for so long that it seemed impossible that the stores could still be so full. What treasures *were* across that border, only ten or twelve miles away from here?

He went back to Nathan Road; for the first time he would have been glad of a rickshaw, but none was in sight; nor was a taxi. If he wasn't careful he would be late. He began to quicken his step, afraid that he might have to walk all the way, trying to remember how to get to Brabazon's headquarters; he had not walked there before, and he knew that the shopping district was a maze of narrow streets.

A rickshaw boy who looked in his sixties appeared out of a doorway.

"Like nice long ride, gentleman?"

"I'd like a quick ride," said Mannering. "How much to the police headquarters in Chatham Road?"

"Five Hong Kong dollars, sir."

"Ten if you get me there in ten minutes."

Within two minutes Mannering almost regretted the offer; he had not realised that a rickshaw could be so uncomfortable, or could be drawn so fast by an old man. No one appeared to take any notice of them, and the police watch was out of sight; he sat holding on, half afraid of being thrown out, half afraid that this man had been trailing him and would take him to the wrong place.

In seven minutes exactly they pulled up outside police headquarters. The rickshaw boy was gasping for breath, sweat was pouring down his face. Mannering felt a sharp twinge of compunction, took out a twenty-dollar note and handed it to him, and then went into headquarters. He was five minutes early, but Brabazon and Lovelace were waiting in Brabazon's office. The whisky and the gin and the beer were already going the rounds, and Brabazon gave him the impression that he was desperately on edge. After Mannering reported in detail, the policeman said:

"The truth is if we get them both to agree we'll have them talking, and it hardly ever happens," he said. "What impression did Hanno give you? He's a crafty old devil, and——"

His telephone bell rang.

"Can't be him," he exclaimed. "He wouldn't be early." He watched as Lovelace plucked up the telephone, and a moment later the Superintendent held the instrument out to him.

"Dooley," he announced.

"Ah, yes, he's anxious too.... Hallo, Sam.... No, not yet, but don't expect miracles, will you? ... Yes, he's here ... my dear chap, you can be sure we'll look after him, last man in the world we want to lose.... I'll call you." He rang off, and gave a curious kind of barking laugh. "He told me to look after you! Apparently he doesn't know how good you are at looking after yourself. I——"

The bell rang again.

A moment later, Lovelace said: "For you, Mr. Mannering." As he handed over the instrument, he nodded to Brabazon, who moved his position a little and then stood with his whisky glass in his hand.

154

"Mr. Mannering," said Dr. Hanno, in his most courteous voice, "I have now been able to discuss this matter with my colleagues and I am happy to tell you that they agree with me, that in these special circumstances we should assist in the most difficult and delicate task of protecting this precious heritage. If you will be good enough to ask Sir Hugh to get in touch with me, I will be glad to arrange the details."

"Would you like to talk to him now, sir?" Mannering suggested.

"If he is available, then yes, by all means."

Lovelace was grinning broadly. Brabazon raised both hands above his head, clasped and shook them like a boxer acknowledging the plaudits of the crowd, then snatched up the receiver. "Dr. Hanno," he said, in a voice that Mannering hardly recognised, "I am very glad to talk to you again. . . . Yes, the utmost security. . . . Yes, I suppose so, in the circumstances." He frowned, and sat on a corner of his desk, looking for a moment as if he had come upon some snag, and anxiety began to flood back into Mannering's mind. "I understand," Brabazon said. "But not officially, you understand. . . . Yes. . . . I see no objection to that. . . . How many men? . . . Forty should be ample, we shall then have two hundred men on guard. . . . Yes, tomorrow morning, I'll arrange for everyone to have a briefing session together. . . . Yes, everyone. . . . Yes." He grinned. "I'll make sure of that. Yes, sir. . . . Good night."

He rang off, brushed his hands over his hair and then pressed the heels of his palms against his forehead; Mannering had come to recognise that as a characteristic gesture. Half chuckling, he said:

"He wants us to make sure that we don't let his group get at the other Chinese group—the old devil actually has a sense of humour!" The smile gradually faded. He frowned, beat his forehead for a few seconds so heavily that Mannering heard the thuds, then he dropped his hands to his sides and went on in a deep, more authoritative voice: "He also says that he wants the Press to say that all the security men will shoot to kill." Brabazon frowned at Mannering. "Hope we haven't done something we'll regret," he added. "Well, no use anticipating trouble. I'd better have a talk to the General."

As he picked up the telephone again, Lovelace said in a hard voice:

"Everyone will shoot to kill all right. I wouldn't like to be the one to try to break into the Ho Sun Gallery."

20
FULL SECURITY

MANNERING stepped out of the police car outside the Peninsular Hotel just before midnight. He had been with the Brabazons for dinner, and he had learned that Lady Brabazon was fully aware of what was going on. Brabazon was jumping up and down for the telephone all the evening, but his wife kept up a running fire of comment and conversation, mostly about contrasts between here and London.

"And the moment Mrs. Mannering arrives you are to get in touch with me," she once said. "I can give her a dozen wrinkles about the best way to shop, and where to go without spending a fortune. I'd love to show her round, too—I don't do a lot of shopping myself but it's always a thrill to help someone else spend their money."

Or:

"Did you see last Tuesday's London *Times*? It gets here only two days late, one day sometimes, but I get lazier and lazier, and I only looked through it this afternoon. I'd no idea that Mrs. Mannering had such a reputation. Fancy her having twelve of her paintings in the London Gallery, and being an R.A.—do you think she would be prepared to paint Hugh? I've always wanted a good portrait of him, a photograph somehow never catches the real man. It makes him too handsome." She smiled up at her husband as he came from the

156

telephone for what must have been the sixth time. "Doesn't it, dear?"

"Handsome is as handsome does," said Brabazon gruffly. He dropped into his chair, and a Chinese man-servant brought more roast beef from the hot plate, and placed it beside him. "John, everyone thought yours was a damned good idea when it *was* an idea, but now it's all practical politics they're chasing each other in circles, scared of what will happen if anything goes wrong."

"By 'going wrong' you mean a clash between the two Chinese security guards, dear, don't you?" Lady Brabazon sounded as if honey wouldn't melt in her mouth.

"You know what I mean. That was the Governor, wanting to make sure that I've taken all possible security measures! Ought to have banned the show, that's the truth of it, then there wouldn't be all this fuss. Mind you, I'm not blaming you," he added to Mannering.

"Nice of you," murmured Mannering.

"Hugh, I think John is the most patient and long-suffering man alive. I really do. Ever since he's been here you've made it clear that you are blaming him, whereas it's nothing to do with him. After all, you asked him to help. It's a good thing someone managed to prod you into doing something, too, because you've been saying for months, in fact for years, that the things stored in Hong Kong for Americans who can't take them home have been like a powder-keg. Your do-nothing policy hasn't made it any less dangerous, now at least there's a chance of preventing it from blowing up. Don't take any notice of him, John." She was the merriest and most chubby little thing, round-faced, looking ten years younger than her forty-three years, fluffy-haired, pink-cheeked; she wore a peach-coloured dress which didn't really suit her and yet in a way was exactly right.

"Even my wife joins forces against me," Brabazon complained. "The worst of it is, she's right. Not often she is, but this time she's bang on the nose. We've dithered about this business, not wanting to offend anybody—our cardinal sin is

157

being frightened it might upset one of the Chinas, or the U.S.A., or some tinpot little Eastern potentate who—oh, hell, *no*!"

The telephone bell was ringing again in a small ante-room. He pushed his chair back and stamped out. Lady Brabazon watched him, showing more concern now than she had all the evening.

"I'm afraid he *is* worried," she reflected. "But this has simply brought it to a head, and when it's over he'll thank you."

Mannering laughed.

"Or hate the sight of me, but that won't matter much. I shan't be here for long!"

Brabazon came back almost at once; grinning.

"Someone's happy," he announced. "That was Dooley, to say he's had a reply from Washington telling him to use his own judgment. No one said anything about the Yanks shooting to kill, I suppose we ought to be thankful for small mercies."

These things were passing through Mannering's mind as he went into the hotel. Several suitcases were standing by the front door, bearing B.O.A.C. labels, but he did not give them a second thought. He looked around, half hoping that Christiansen or Vansitter would be in the lounge, but neither was. He saw a dealer from Sydney whom he knew slightly, and another from Paris, but both were with youngish-looking women and he did not let them see him.

It was nearly one o'clock when he went to bed in a room on the seventh floor, immediately below the one he had had upstairs, and identical except for the pattern of the tapestry covering of the settee and two chairs. He did not waste time getting into bed; Hong Kong seemed to have an enervating effect on him, and he had been yawning all the way home in the car. He knew that the window was being watched from the street, and that there was a police guard at the door. There was no need to fear another raid.

He woke a little after seven o'clock, of his own accord. No one was knocking, the telephone was silent, the only sound was from the railway station opposite the hotel. He rang for tea, decided to breakfast in the dining-room, wondered whether Brabazon had had an undisturbed night—and then opened the door to his room boy. On the tea tray was a copy of the *South China Post*, and the front page headline screamed:

GUARDS TO SHOOT TO KILL

Fantastic Security Plans for Fabulous Collection

There wasn't much more to the story than the headline, although it gave some details of the treasures, and a potted history of the Ho Sun Gallery. When Mannering went down to breakfast he looked about for one of the other dealers; none was in sight. He took his time over the meal and relished the service, then strolled downstairs, a little at a loose end. There were no messages, presumably it had been a quiet night; certainly he would have heard had there been a raid on the gallery. He went downstairs to see if there was any post; there was none. He moved to the next desk, and asked:

"Can you give me Mr. Christiansen's room number?"

A rather earnest, shiny-faced young man with huge horn-rimmed glasses looked apologetically, and said:

"Mr. Christiansen is no longer with us, sir. He left last night."

Mannering could hardly believe his hears.

"He took one o'clock aeroplane. It was delayed because of some engine trouble," went on the clerk. "I am very sorry, sir."

"Is Mr. Vansitter still here?" Mannering inquired, but he felt that he already knew the answer.

"No, sir, Mr. Vansitter left also on the same aeroplane," the clerk said. "Both had telegrams, recalling them."

*   *   *

"Yes, we knew they'd both left," Lovelace told Mannering on the telephone. "Each man had a cable just before he took

159

off—there was a fire at one man's home or shop, and a robbery at the other."

"I'd like to know if they were summoned from home, or whether something which happened here scared them off," said Mannering, and added almost to himself: "And I'd like to know what it's all about." When Lovelace made no reply, Mannering went on in the same thoughtful tone: "Who wants to make sure that no experts see that collection?"

"*What?*"

"You heard me."

Lovelace gave a brusque little laugh.

"Yes. Just. I should have thought it was obvious."

"What's so obvious?" asked Mannering.

"Someone wants to make sure that there are no dealers here to buy any of the goods in the exhibition. If there is no show of outside interest and the things are left in Hong Kong, it will quicken the competition between the two governments."

"H'm." Mannering was non-committal. "I'm not sure I follow that argument, but I would still like to know what was in the cables those men received, and also whether any of the other dealers who were here yesterday have returned."

"Give me an hour," pleaded Lovelace. "It's a hell of a morning. We wanted to concentrate everything we could on the Ho Sun Gallery, but every kind of bad man is busy in Hong Kong today. We raided a junk which had come down from Singapore—the hull was choc-a-bloc with crude opium." He paused. "They refine it, and it's worth a pound an ounce. They ship it across to the West coast of America where it becomes worth anything up to a thousand dollars an ounce. We've had a sudden burst of activity on the New Territory frontier post, too—another flood of refugees are coming in from Red China. This could be a deliberate diversion to prevent us from giving Ho Sun's gallery full security, but we've plenty of military, once we're organised. Supposing I give you a chit, and you go along to the cable office and find out what was in those cables."

"I'd like that," said Mannering.

*   *   *

The cable to Christiansen said: *"Shop raided last night considerable loss by theft and damage advise your immediate return."*

The cable to Vansitter said: *"Serious fire in basement damage over two fifty grand please come home."*

*   *   *

Mannering walked away from the offices of the cable company, near the new port terminal, with copies of the cables in his pocket, together with copies to the Ho brothers and two more of the dealers. He would not have thought it possible that he could stride through the streets of Kowloon taking no notice of anything in the windows and almost oblivious of the picturesque streets, but he noticed hardly a thing. As he turned into a street within sight of the triangular premises of the Li Chen brothers' Kowloon shop, he saw four uniformed policemen, two soldiers, and several plainclothes men close to the windows; this was the first evidence of full security. Policemen were in sight farther along the street, too.

Madame Li Chen and Raymond were in the shop; there was no sign of the older brother, but two Chinese youths were at the back of the main counter, cleaning a display case. The Li Chens came forward quickly, almost eagerly, and Mannering had a feeling that Raymond had to bite back the first words which came to mind, and force himself to say bitterly:

"At least you are still with us, Mr. Mannering."

"So you know who's gone," said Mannering.

"Each of them was courteous enough to leave a message for us," said Raymond Li Chen. He picked up a little sheaf of notes from a small desk, and held them out. "What has happened to them is what happened to you in London—every effort has been made to make sure that they do not visit the exhibition, and that they do not buy from me. If it were not being done on such an enormous scale, I would begin to believe that this was simply an effort to ruin me."

161

His wife said: "Mr. Mannering, answer me, please. Have you come to tell us that you are going back to London?"

"No," said Mannering. "Not until the exhibition is over, anyhow." The relief in the woman's face seemed quite remarkable. "I came to see if you knew about these, that's all. Have the Hos returned?"

"They are still in Kowloon, with two other dealers who do not have very much influence, and who are here, one might say, as a tax manoeuvre," answered Raymond. "They are none the less welcome, but—Mr. Mannering, you are the only true expert in antiques and *objets d'art* left in Hong Kong. I have no desire to alarm you, but—are you positive that every precaution has been taken to make sure of your safety? If anything were now to happen to you, it would be the most tragic time of my life."

*　　　*　　　*

There was something wrong with his approach to this case, Mannering thought; from the beginning he had felt frustrated, as if he had no freedom to act for himself, and up to a point it was still true. His mind would not work properly, except in flashes of perception. He had been so obsessed by the effect of the latest withdrawals from the Li Chens that he had not thought seriously about the obvious danger to himself. Every attempt had been made to keep him away from here. There had been the one raid which might well have ended in his death, and yet the evidence was clear: someone wanted to make sure that none of the would-be buyers saw the exhibition. If this policy were carried to the obvious conclusion, then another attempt was likely soon to keep him away; and the obvious form of such an attempt would be to kill him. He needed no telling that this was in the minds of the two Chinese who stood in the middle of this beautiful shop, surrounded by rare and precious things. He was vividly aware of the moment when he had seen the "bomb" hurtling towards the window. Was it possible that there would be another bold attack?

Obviously, Brabazon and Lovelace half expected one on the

shop; did they also expect one on him? It was one thing to be shadowed by the police as a security measure, another to feel that these precautions were being taken because the authorities felt sure that he would be attacked.

"Mr. Mannering, I am sorry indeed if I have alarmed you," said Raymond Li Chen softly. "But you appear to be so oblivious of danger that I felt that I must try to make you aware of it. I would like to make a suggestion, please. Instead of waiting until tonight, come earlier to the Ho Sun Gallery, so that nothing can happen to prevent you from going."

After a moment or two, Mannering asked: "When will you be there?"

"I shall return at once. I came here this morning only because my wife told me of these messages. My brother Charles is supervising the final arrangements at the exhibition. Will you come, Mr. Mannering?"

21

THE TREASURE HOUSE

MANNERING said slowly, almost painfully: "I would like to come early, but not yet." When Raymond bowed his acceptance of that decision, Mannering went on, trying to keep pace with his thoughts: "Have you been there this morning?"

"Yes, of course. We live on the island, not far from the Ho Sun Gallery. In the past ten days, while the goods have been taken there, I have spent more time in the galleries than in my shop—except of course for the short time that I was in Bombay. Why do you ask?"

"Are the security precautions in hand?"

"Yes," said Raymond, nodding. His puffy eyes were rather swollen, and he stared at Mannering through sparse spiky lashes; he gave the impression that he was also trying to probe what was going on in Mannering's mind. "They are excellent. Two hundred men are on duty, in or around the gallery at all times. Each contingent is on guard for four hours, then rests, then takes over again for another four hours. Three senior Army officers, two senior policemen, two American military attachés as well as representatives from the two governments are there. When I saw all that I told myself that it was quite impossible for any successful attack to be made, and yet—I would have thought that other things that have happened were impossible too."

"So no one at all can get in without a pass."

"And the police are co-operating with my brother, in issuing those. Mr. Mannering, be careful, please. Be *very* careful."

Raymond Li Chen's wife moved forward and touched Mannering's hand, but she did not speak.

Mannering left the shop almost immediately, and walked towards Nathan Road. It was a relief to know that he was followed by two policemen whom he recognised, but now he had a more urgent sense of danger—as if an assassin were waiting for him at every corner and in every doorway. A little man with big ears which jutted out came towards him, earnest in manner, and Mannering felt a stab of alarm.

"I recommend velly good tailor, sir, come this way, please."

"No," Mannering said harshly. He thrust his way forward as the little man stood back and gaped. Mannering reached Nathan Road, making sure that his bodyguard was close behind him. It was as if he had been asleep for a long time, and had only just become aware of the deadly danger.

Every expert had been lured away from the exhibition except him, and whoever was behind these crimes knew that he would not be lured away, so the obvious thing was——

He heard a shout, from behind. He spun round. He saw the taller of the two policemen flinging himself forward. He heard the sharp crack of a shot. He felt the policeman's hands at his ankles, exactly as hands had tugged at him on the pier. He crashed down. Falling, he felt sharp, stinging pains in his ankles and in one leg above the knee. People screamed, and footsteps thudded, a car horn hooted, there were two more sharp reports followed almost simultaneously by a loud report, nearer and frightening. Immediately afterwards glass smashed, and Mannering knew that a window had been struck by a bullet. Apart from gasping sounds, as of people who had been running, and footsteps and far away traffic there was quiet when slowly he picked himself up.

Then he saw an awful thing.

The policeman who had pulled him out of danger had a bloody hole in the back of his head; he lay on his face, completely still; and Mannering needed no telling that in fact he had been killed.

*   *   *

Brabazon and Lovelace were together in the Commissioner's office when Mannering rached there, twenty minutes later. By then the dead man's body had been removed in an ambulance, and a squad of police and military were searching the area for the gunman. The second policeman who had been watching Mannering had reported that both of them had seen a man on a roof, pointing a rifle; that was why the now dead officer had shouted a warning.

"Sooner or later we'll get the swine," growled Brabazon. "But it will probably be later, and we need results now." He drew in a rasping breath. "Sure you're not hurt?"

"A few chippings from the pavement stung me, that's all," said Mannering. "I didn't see the sharpshooter. I almost wish your chaps hadn't, either." When Brabazon simply pressed his hands against his forehead and Lovelace shrugged, he went on: "I know one thing now."

Lovelace asked: "What's that?"

Both of these men were badly shaken, both men hated the fact that one of their policemen had been killed. It was a good thing to see that they were so distressed; it would be bad indeed if they allowed that to affect their actions or their judgment.

"I want more than ever to see that collection," Mannering said.

165

"We can make sure that no one gets inside the galleries, we can make sure you're safe when you're actually on the lawns approaching it," said Brabazon, taking his hands away. "We can't be sure that someone else won't take a potshot at you. Do you know what I think? I think you ought to be confined to a room here, or a room at the hotel, where you can be guarded so that no one can possibly get at you. If they get you after all this, it would be naked defeat. Don't make any mistake about it—it wouldn't simply be a case of wounded pride or loss of prestige, it would make it look as if the British weren't able to look after the Colony properly. It could be disastrous."

"Even if it were as bad as that, I'd still say that I've got to get into those galleries and check on the genuineness of the goods in the exhibition," Mannering said stubbornly. "According to Raymond Li Chen there isn't another consultant here who could do it."

"There are dozens of experts in Hong Kong!"

"Unprejudiced, unbiased, and proof against corruption?" asked Mannering.

"Hugh," said Lovelace, forsaking formality in this tension, "I think he's right."

"I know he's right," Brabazon said, just as sharply as Mannering. "What I don't know is whether we can get him to the exhibition alive. Don't make any mistake about it, this place is so swarming with Chinese that it isn't possible to watch every spot, it isn't possible to make sure that someone on a ferry, on a launch, in a sampan, even a skin diver or a rickshaw man, doesn't have another go. The Chinese know this place like the palms of their hands, and if they mean to stop Mannering getting to the galleries the odds are against getting him there."

Lovelace said: "If I know Mannering, he'll take the chance."

"Well, I'm not sure that I ought to let him."

"I think you're making too much of this," Mannering interpolated. "There shouldn't be any serious danger if they don't know who I am. All I need is a uniform to fit me, and an hour with what Lovelace calls my box of tricks. No one can be familiar with all the officers here. If it comes to a point I could be an Army officer. All I need is a permit to go through into the galleries as one of the security forces."

Brabazon now stood very still, with his back to the window, and Lovelace was smiling in that crooked way he had.

"They'll know the police officers," he said, "but they can't know all the Army chaps. We can fix it, Hugh."

"One other thing," Mannering said.

"What's that?"

"Apart from us and one or two Army officers, no one should know what I'm doing," Mannering said.

"I couldn't agree more," Brabazon assured him. "But John, don't fool yourself, will you? Whatever precautions we take and however careful we are there's still a grave risk."

"Let's say I still think you exaggerate," Mannering said, with much more confidence than he felt. "If you can arrange for two or three officers to come here in one car, and to slip in quickly so that no one watching gets a good look at them, I can go out as one of them and the other chap can stay here until after dark. And I'll need my make-up box from the hotel. It's still in James C. Mason's room."

"We'll do that," Brabazon promised, and turned to Lovelace. "Arrange it, Mike." Then he looked levelly at Mannering and asked: "Do you suspect anyone?"

"Yes, of course."

"Who?"

"The Li Chens."

Brabazon began to breathe hard through his nostrils.

"You mean you think they're fakes, and the Li Chens don't mean to allow any experts to see them?"

"I don't know what the motives are," said Mannering. "It's been fairly obvious for some time that this was someone with limited manpower to call on, and that wouldn't be true of government-sponsored attacks. The man who attacked me in the bath had raided Li Chen's gallery only an hour or so earlier, quite probably an attempt to mislead us. Someone who

167

knew who had been invited in the first place did all the cancelling to keep other dealers away and send Christiansen back to London. Raymond Li Chen is almost certainly involved. It's been obvious—or it's seemed obvious—that experts were being kept away, and——"

"The only logical reason is that the so-called treasures are fakes," interrupted Brabazon. "Can you check in a short time?"

"I can check," Mannering said. "But there could be two logical explanations, you know."

*   *   *

It was a long time since Mannering had been in the uniform of a captain in the British Army; it seemed an age and was in fact nearly twenty years. The uniform borrowed from a captain in the Royal Engineers fitted him reasonably well, and he did not fear that anyone would notice that the trousers were a trifle short and the sleeves of the coat an inch or so short, too. He felt more conspicuous in the uniform than he had as Mason or as himself; it was as if everyone was staring at him and the three officers who left the police station with him, early in the afternoon. One was Captain Oliver, also in the Royal Engineers, the others were lieutenants in the East London Regiment, then stationed in Hong Kong. As far as Mannering could judge, no one followed them to the ferry. They climbed out of a jeep one after another, the three genuine officers all younger than Mannering, and went briskly towards the entrance gates, paid their ten cents, and pushed their way one at a time past the turnstile. Dozens of people thronged the entrance gates, which were closed. As Mannering's party reached the back of the crowd, the gates opened. A ferry was being tied alongside by a man who looked too old and too tired to wear any kind of uniform; the rope he used was thicker than his wrist. The crowd thronged forward. Mannering felt himself jostled from all sides, and realised how easy an attack would be. Any one of dozens of Chinese could stick a knife in his ribs. No one seemed remotely interested in him, only in

168

getting a seat. The engine was throbbing, and the big ferry swaying up and down. Hundreds upon hundreds of people poured on board, until every seat was taken. A bell clanged, gates closed, the ferry began to move almost on the instant. All this was done with a slickness and precision which astonished Mannering, even taking his thoughts off the immediate problem.

They soon came back.

He looked about the faces and the heads around him. Here and there, sitting alongside the Chinese, was a European. In one place a dozen, obviously from one of the ships in the docks, were staring with awe and fascination at the harbour scene. The water was choppy and small boats were bobbing up and down, some of them coming so close that it was almost as if they were about to attack. An even larger ferry, packed with people and with cars, crossed their bows, with only feet to spare, but no one seemed concerned.

"Better get moving," said the youngest officer, who wasn't long out of his teens. They all stood up, but as the ferry drew alongside the island terminal, every other passenger seemed to stand up and make a beeline for the doors; it looked as if there was no hope of them going through smoothly, but they seemed to be swallowed up, and there was no great crush. Mannering looked about him, not seriously on edge for himself. The terminal was much newer on this side than on the other, and there were some modern buildings straight ahead, some wide driveways which carried private cars and taxis. A jeep was parked alongside the taxi rank, and a young sergeant sprang to attention as they reached him.

"I'll drive," said one of the lieutenants. "Wait here for instructions, sergeant."

"Very good, sir!"

"The quickest way seems to be the most attractive," said Captain Oliver. "Like a Cook's Tour?"

"Later," said Mannering.

"Right."

The lieutenant drove towards the main street, where a row

169

of trams was lined up, dark-green anachronisms to any eye fresh from England. Traffic was thick on both sides of the tramlines, the pavements were so crowded that everyone appeared to be walking along at the same pace, carried along by his neighbours. Tram gongs clanged, horns blew, nonchalant-looking Chinese policemen controlled the traffic as if they had all the time in the world. Mannering looked up towards the left, seeing the narrow streets which rose so steeply towards the top of a hill which seemed to reach the pale-blue skyline. On either side were stalls so full of colour and overfull of goods for sale that there seemed no room for anyone to walk; and along these narrow streets there was no motor traffic, although a few cyclists were precariously weaving their way down. Every head in sight seemed to be Chinese. At one corner, a little old woman was sitting on a stool, with a younger woman brushing her hair until it shone like a black mirror. The impressions of colour, of bustle, of plenty, were vivid and yet hopelessly confused in Mannering's mind.

They reached a wider point in the road, and traffic moved more freely.

"Won't be long now, sir," said the lieutenant.

The road now ran uphill. On either side were private houses, not shops, and the higher they went the larger these houses became. All of them stood in their own grounds, all gave Mannering something of the impression of the French Riviera houses at the end of the season. Now and again he caught a glimpse of the harbour, and of Kowloon across the water, but it was gone in a flash.

They came to a gateway, on the right. By this were six men—a policeman, a British soldier, an American sailor, and two Chinese in unfamiliar uniforms. A British policeman came out of a small sentry box, saluted, and said:

"Your passes, please."

Each man in the jeep had a pass, and each had to show it before they were allowed through. To Mannering it seemed as if the grounds were bristling with armed men, each bush and each tree seemed to conceal a gun. The drive through the trees was only about two hundred yards along, and they came out into open grassland, dotted here and there with trees and bushes, but none was enough to give cover. Beyond, on the side of the hill, were the Ho Sun Galleries, and had they been designed as a military defence post they could not have been better sited. Lining the road, and in different places about the parkland, were policemen and military in pairs; now and again Mannering noticed two more of the white-clad American sailors.

They drew up outside the main doors.

Mannering climbed down, as Lovelace himself approached, with another Army captain. There was a little flurry of saluting, before Captain Oliver said:

"We've come to check the internal arrangements. Will you come with us, Superintendent?"

"I'd like to," Lovelace said. "Thanks." The other guards drew aside, and Mannering was among the first of the group to step inside the galleries.

As he did so, for the first time he began to appreciate the size and the scope of this exhibition. One long gallery, at least a hundred yards from this door to another at the far side, was huge and spacious, and in its way quite beautiful. Curved glass, some of it stained, some of it clear, rounded off the top corners of this gallery, so that everything on show was perfectly illuminated in daylight; and great lanterns of silk and precious metal hung from the ceiling, giving promise of ample light by night. Along each wall were alcoves, and in each alcove something of great beauty, and four wide arches were on either side, leading to other sections of the gallery.

It was like stepping into a treasure house of the ages; into all the magnificence of the east.

22

THE WAY OF ATTACK

As he stood studying the arrangement of the long gallery while trying not to be side-tracked by the glittering beauty of the scene, Mannering realised that there were at least twenty guards on duty here—stationed at points of vantage, including every doorway and every archway. There was no doubt that this had been handled as a military operation, and no shadow of doubt that Brabazon feared that a raid would be attempted.

As well as guards, there were workmen. Most of these were in shapeless cotton trousers and billowing jackets, two actually with pigtails. Two men, better dressed than the others, were polishing a statue of a Buddha made of gold and marble. Another was dusting a small pagoda, standing about waist high; it looked as if it were of beaten gold, with clusters of precious stones as gables, and a door of diamonds. Mannering had seen pictures of it, and knew that it was nearly a thousand years old.

He walked with the others in military precision along the main passage. It was like walking through a hall of ancient days, as if the craftsmen and the artists of all China had given of their heart and their minds to create such things. Even the archways had been used as part of the exhibition; each one was a carved gateway, a *p'ai lou* of marble, of silver, of lacquered wood or of gold.

Mannering did not stop at any single exhibit, but appeared to study the guards, all of whom were standing at attention; even the policemen were affected by the military bearing of the others. The footsteps of the four men rang out sharply. They turned into the first gateway, and here they were in a hall of armour and of jewelled swords, of spears and knives, like an armoury of an age of emperors.

One of the other officers said under his breath:

"How long will you need on your own?" It was Oliver.

172

"Probably an hour," Mannering replied. "We'll clear one of the side galleries when I've had a chance to look at them all." It was strange to march along, as if the statues and the paintings, the vases and the sculptures of dragons and of gods were on parade, being inspected with the brisk, aloof appraisal of the four military men.

The second side gallery, approached through a *p'ai lou* of black and vermilion lacquer, was filled with lacquered wood, the third with religious sculptures, the fourth with porcelain and enamelled vases, some of them of a shape and a beauty which seemed to affect even Mannering's companions. No one spoke while they were on their rounds. The workmen, standing here and there and appraising, or else putting the finishing touches to the polish or the position of the exhibits, took little notice of them; everyone seemed absorbed in what he was doing.

At the marble gateway of the last of the eight side galleries was a recess, and at the recess a table with small cabinets surrounding it. One of the cabinets was open, and Mannering saw that these were card indexes, listing the contents of the exhibition. He felt a little bemused by the prodigality of the treasures, and for a moment he did not recognise Charles Li Chen, who was sitting at the desk. When he did, he almost made the fatal mistake of acknowledging him; his lips actually parted.

"What is this?" he asked in a voice no one who knew him would recognise.

"This is the information desk," Oliver stated. "I was there this morning." Charles Li Chen was on his feet, smiling his mask of a smile. On the desk was a book, open at the middle, and Mannering saw a pile of similar books on the floor near him. He noticed a page-sized coloured print of one of the pagodas, and realised belatedly that these were catalogues. He nodded at Li Chen, and said to the lieutenant: "I would like one of the catalogues." As he waited, he went on: "I'm satisfied that there is no hiding-place here which is not under surveillance." And that was true. "But of course the galleries are vulnerable to two kinds of attack."

173

Captain Oliver exclaimed: "Two?"

"What's that?" asked Lovelace.

Mannering moved out of Charles Li Chen's earshot, and said grimly: "I hope it hasn't been overlooked—no, it can't have been."

"If you'd tell me what you're talking about, I could tell you," said Oliver. Underneath his calm exterior there was evidence of strain, and the sarcasm was clear in his voice.

"One well-aimed bomb," Mannering said. "A dozen well-aimed fire-bombs—from the air, of course."

"We don't believe that an air attack is practicable," said Oliver. He was small, dark-haired, precise, a little over-confident, almost arrogant. "The only places it can come from are the Colony itself, and every spot from which a plane could take off is watched—every plane is spotted, anyhow—or the Chinese mainland, and that's hardly likely, because if one came from there we would know that it was with the authority of Peking, and they don't want to cause an incident any more than we do. There's Macao, the Portuguese Colony, but we are in close liaison with the Portuguese commander in charge of military forces, and will be advised of all aircraft leaving the territory, or from a vessel at sea. Which one do you think is more likely?"

"I'd say Macao," said Mannering, ignoring the sarcasm. "There are regular air services to and from the Colony, aren't there? Only one aircraft with one bomb would be necessary." He felt as if the years had dropped away and he was discussing military dangers when in a bridgehead in Normandy after D-Day. "A plane could get through, and even if it were reported flying off course there wouldn't be any time to stop it."

"There would be plenty of time to make sure it couldn't be flown away," said Oliver, and Lovelace looked his agreement. "I doubt if they will take that risk."

Mannering said: "They've taken a lot of risks already." There was no point in arguing with the man, and at heart he doubted the probability of such an attack; he simply felt oppressed by a menace he could not identify. "The only other

174

way of causing serious damage would be from a time-bomb hidden in or beneath the galleries."

"Every square inch has been searched by our sappers and a bomb-disposal unit, using mine detectors," Captain Oliver said. "I really think you can take it for granted that all the normal precautions have been taken."

"I can vouch for the fact that every vase, everything which could be used to hide incendiary material has been searched," put in Lovelace. "We have done this kind of thing before, you know."

"I should have thought that was obvious," said Oliver, acidly. "I had not realised that you were coming here to overlook the security arrangements."

"Just the outsider with the fresh approach," Mannering replied equably. "And also with a lifetime of experience with this kind of art, which should help to find out whether it's genuine or not. Some of it is, undoubtedly," he went on in a subdued voice. "No one could copy those *p'ai lou,* or gateways, some of the carving certainly goes back to the twelfth or thirteenth century. But they go with the galleries, I presume, and no one is likely to want to take them away, although they might like to claim insurance if they were damaged. I'd very much like to spend half an hour in the fourth gallery annexe on the right—could we have a special search there so that no one knows what I'm after?"

Oliver, a little taken aback, said: "Yes, I suppose so."

"Did you see something there?" asked Lovelace.

"It's the one place where I can examine a dozen or more small things and check their genuineness," said Mannering. "The jewels on the seated Bodhisattva, for instance, if they're genuine they're beyond price. It's T'ang Dynasty, and only two were jewelled—in India, I was told, and brought back by missionary priests in about A.D. 800. It's impossible to tell at a cursory glance. And there's a Sung dynasty vase with a tiny chip on the neck which should enable me to see how deep and approximately how old the glazing is. If genuine, it's about A.D. 1000."

175

Oliver moistened his lips. Lovelace said: "I'll tell Charles Li Chen what we're going to do." He moved towards the information desk and as he reached it, a door behind the man opened and Raymond Li Chen came in, dressed exactly as Mannering had last seen him. Two of their assistants were within earshot, and Lovelace talked in Chinese. The Li Chens raised no objections. The little group of officers walked towards the fourth annexe, with Raymond Li Chen ahead, calling out to the workmen who stopped what they were doing at the word of command. The annexe was completely empty of people when Mannering and the others reached there. Raymond Li Chen stood beneath a magnificent silver, gold, and lacquer gateway, holding three of the catalogues in his hand.

"Will you be good enough to place these on the tables," he said to Lovelace. "We are getting very near to the official opening time."

Lovelace took them. "Yes."

"Thank you. May I ask what special reason you have for examining this gallery, Superintendent?"

"We think that some of the floor mosaic has been disturbed lately, and we want to check," said Lovelace.

"I cannot believe——" Raymond began, but he broke off before saying more quietly: "You are right to take every precaution. If you are also right about the floor, then the staff of the museum must surely be involved. Gentlemen, the guests for the opening will soon be leaving their homes. I hope it will not be necessary to keep them waiting outside."

"So do I," said Lovelace non-committally.

"One other thing——"

"We must get busy," Oliver interrupted sharply.

"You are indeed right," said Raymond, "but allow me just one other question, Superintendent. Do you know if Mr. Mannering is coming?"

"Not if we can keep him away," Lovelace said harshly.

Raymond looked astonished, and for once his face showed exactly what he thought.

"Why do you say that?"

176

"He was attacked and nearly killed by a sharp-shooter from the roof of the new Island View Hotel," Lovelace answered. "He wants to come, but the Commissioner has so far refused to allow it. I doubt whether he will be here. We don't want a prominent British citizen murdered in Hong Kong."

"I am shocked, deeply shocked," said Raymond. He bowed, and moved away.

The group of officers went forward. Oliver gave a word of command and six of his men formed a cordon across the gateway which led to the annexe, two of Lovelace's men moved some museum assistants who could see what was going on. Mannering took out a watchmaker's glass and a diamond cutter, went straight to the statue of the Bodhisattva and knelt in front of it as if he were paying homage. The statue was about two feet high, beautifully sculptured, with a necklace of diamonds inlaid in the stone. If these were faked, then he would make a mark on them with just a touch of the cutter.

The sun, reflecting from several panes of glass, fell upon the side of the statue and the necklace, and as Mannering knelt beside it, a thousand scintillas of brilliant light seemed to stab out from the diamonds, quite dazzling him. He felt a strange attraction, almost as if the breath was being drawn out of him. Precious stones had this physical effect on him, as if he were allergic to them. He had never felt like this with false jewels. He saw the absolute perfection of the setting, and he knew that it must have taken months for these jewels to be set, whether they were real or fake—and who would spend so much time on paste diamonds?

He was aware of Oliver almost breathing down his neck and Lovelace approaching from the far end of the annexe, where he had put one of the catalogues. Mannering found himself breathing in short, sharp gasps. He knew that Oliver was aware of this and would wonder what was the matter with him, and why he did not move. He made himself raise his right hand, steady the statue with his left hand, and place the diamond cutter on a diamond at the top of the neck, only just below the ear. He slashed it, twice. He knew that if these were

177

paste then a tiny trail of powder would show, no fake diamond was proof against this particular edge.

There was no sign of powder; no mark at all.

Oliver exclaimed: "Well?"

"They're real," said Mannering unsteadily. The flashes of light caught in the sun, the sheer brilliance of the necklace, the knowledge that these diamonds were genuine, affected him almost too much. He made himself test two more, with the same result, then stood up and said gruffly: "I'll look at that Sung vase." He crossed to it, a deep red-coloured vase standing three feet high, taking out the watchmaker's glass. Again the sun helped, shining directly on to the neck of the vase, where that tiny chip was open to view. The chip itself was an old one, and had never been repaired. He saw the depths of the glazing, knew that no modern imitation could approach the colour and the texture and the sheen of the vase; it was almost a sacrilege to suspect that it was false.

He drew back. "It's real," he said, more firmly. "I'll have a quick look at a few other things, but I think we'll find they're all genuine." He moved to a set of old ivories, also inlaid with jewels; the diamonds and the rubies were real, beyond doubt. He went to another statue, this time of a woman playing a lute. The pearls in the crown, which was taller than the head itself, had the unmistakable warm lustre of the very real and the very old. He was now as sure as he could be that all the exhibits here were genuine, that whatever reason there had been for keeping the dealers away, it was not to prevent them from discovering that the exhibition was filled with fakes.

Lovelace said in a dry voice: "So that's another notion knocked on the head. How much are these things worth, Captain?"

Mannering said slowly, effortfully: "I can't pretend to guess, but I know that I've seen ten million pounds' worth of jewels and carvings, paintings and sculptures. There must be at least twice as much as that here, and everything is unique. It's the most magnificent collection I've ever seen, it's beyond any single collector's dream, and—it's a crime to break it up.

178

It's more than a cultural treasure house, it's a cultural miracle. And it isn't all Chinese. Some of these came from Bangkok, some from Vietnam, some from Cambodia——"

Across his words, in that moment while everyone near was staring at him, when no one dreamed of danger close by, there was a sharp explosion, loud and clear. Mannering swung round, the others darted their gaze away from him.

Fire was raging at the far end of the annexe, and a dozen, a hundred little fires were dotted about the treasures in this annexe room.

23

THE PENCIL OF FIRE

BEFORE Mannering fully realised what had happened, before the full horror of the danger came to him, Oliver snapped out words of command. Men cordoning the annexe swung round, three of them unslinging what looked like guns from their shoulders—but these were fire-extinguishers. The men worked as if they had been expecting some such thing, moving with speed and precision, touching nothing but squirting the foamy chemical over the fires, putting out one after another. The stink of the chemicals, the smoke from the flames, the stabbing flashes of red where fires still burned, brought men rushing from all over the gallery, some shouting, most open-mouthed in silence. Of the group of officers, only Mannering and Lovelace were by the tiny gold-topped temple which Mannering had last examined.

"How the hell did that start?" Lovelace demanded. "The windows aren't broken, the roof's whole, no one threw any-thing——"

He broke off.

"It started by that table," Mannering said. A small lacquer table still stood at the far end of the annexe, legs buckled,

179

surface almost burnt away. As they stared at it, a soldier squirted foam on it, and hid the top from sight, but not until both men realised the significance. "Those catalogues," breathed Mannering. He stared at one, and saw what he had noticed only subconsciously before—a pencil fitted to each catalogue, as to a pocket diary. "The pencils could——"

"Oliver!" cried Lovelace. "Catalogues—we want to get them all outside! No time for pencils," he muttered to Mannering, and turned and ran towards the main gallery, shouting to his men: "Grab all the catalogues you can. Get them outside!" He snatched one off the nearest table, tried to slip the pencil out, but failed. "Catalogues!" he roared again. He snatched another as he was moving, and Mannering was aware of two things: that at any moment a catalogue might burst into flame, and if it did then any man close by would be severely burned, perhaps burned to death, perhaps blinded. Oliver was calling orders, and only now did he fully appreciate how these men had been trained. A Chinese officer and an American naval lieutenant took up the cry, orders were shouted in two languages. Catalogue after catalogue was snatched up, some men carrying half a dozen.

"Windows!" cried Mannering. "Open the windows."

"*Windows!*" bellowed Oliver.

The museum, which had been so quiet, so beautiful, with a few men standing about, a few working on the finishing touches, was suddenly a seething mass of moving men, mostly in uniform. Windows were flung open, books were carried out, doors were opened, and men rushed into the grounds. Every second Mannering feared that he would hear another explosion and would see a man enveloped in smoke and flame, but there was none. He saw four policemen by the information desk, picking up piles of catalogues.

Raymond Li Chen lay on the floor near by, as if someone had felled him. Charles Li Chen was sitting like an image at the desk where so many catalogues had been.

The thunder of footsteps and the sharp ring of heels on the tiles and the mosaic of the floor was almost gone. The moving

180

men were outside now, most of them still running, but some had already dropped the catalogues and were backing away.

Two British soldiers, catalogues piled so high that some were level with their faces, were running in opposite directions: one man tripped and fell. The catalogues crashed to the ground, and as the man struck it, head towards the books, one of them burst. Mannering saw that the flash and a sheet of flame came from the pencil. Flame and smoke billowed out until the man and the books were enveloped. The other soldier half turned, with the pile still in his arms, then hurled the books away from him like a man tossing a caber, and swung round towards his friend. Smoke and flames nearly hid him from sight, but Mannering saw him clutching for the fallen man's ankles, and drawing him away.

Then there was another explosion ten times louder, and smoke and flame blotted out the whole area, and the two men.

*   *   *

"One thing to be thankful for," Oliver said in a husky voice. "They were the only serious casualties among our chaps. The pencils are miniature contact incendiaries. Fiendish idea."

"A wonderful job," said Lovelace hoarsely. "My God, what a wonderful job."

"The Li Chens——" began Oliver, and turned to look at the two brothers.

Neither of them had moved, except that Charles Li Chen had leaned a little towards one side, so that his head was propped up against a table-lamp; he looked as if he were asleep. So did Raymond. But they were not asleep, they were dead by their own hands. By Raymond's fingers was a small bottle of tablets, and one of the tablets had rolled a few feet away. As Mannering and the others drew nearer there was the unmistakable sickly odour of bitter almonds, proving almost beyond doubt that these men had taken tablets of potassium cyanide, knowing that it was the quickest way to death.

"But *why*?" breathed Oliver.

"There can't be much doubt about it now," said Lovelace in

a subdued voice. "Insurance. If the place had gone up in fire and smoke no one could have proved where the explosions had started—or who put them there. The Li Chens, the manufacturers—anyone who had access to the catalogues. Don't you think so, Mannering?"

"What's that?" Mannering said. "Insurance? I should doubt——" He broke off. "The one person who might be able to tell us is Raymond Li Chen's wife. Will you have her picked up?"

"I've told one of my chaps to telephone the Commissioner to arrange it," Lovelace said. He stood looking about the gallery, where the smoke was dispersing and even the stench was less offensive. "It's two hours to opening time. We could get this place cleared up enough, if we're going to allow the public in, but without the Li Chens, I don't know." He touched his forehead with his hands, a gesture very like Brabazon's. "I'd better check with the boss. Any feeling either way, Mannering?"

"Yes," Mannering said.

"What way then?" Lovelace sounded irritable.

"I think that everyone possible should come and see these treasures," Mannering said. He felt almost as if the diamonds from the neck of the Bodhisattva were emanating their strange power over him. "I think the world ought to see it. Would you like me to talk to Sir Hugh?"

*　　　*　　　*

"Must say I agree with you," said Brabazon, "but I'll have a word with the Governor."

"I think yes," said the Governor, "but it might be wise to have a word with General Suno and Doctor Hanno."

"I would be most disappointed if it were not opened," said the General.

"I myself will be there, of course," said the Doctor.

"Shouldn't think there could be any argument," said Dooley.

*　　　*　　　*

182

"Yes," said the Governor to Brabazon. "Have the galleries cleaned up as much as possible, and when everyone is there I think you'd better make an announcement saying that an attempt was made to burn the place down, and that the Li Chens are dead. No need for more detail yet. Is there any news about Madame Li Chen?"

"She's waiting for me to go and talk to her," said Brabazon. "I think she knows what's happened, but at the moment she isn't saying a word. I think it might be a good idea if Mannering talked to her. They seemed to talk the same kind of language."

"I'll be very interested to hear what she has to say, whoever she talks to," said the Governor. "I shall leave here at five-thirty. Will you be at the galleries?"

"If I'm through here," said Brabazon. He was already lifting another telephone, and almost before he put down one receiver he said into the other: "Oh, Mannering, I wanted a word with you. The Governor and I would be most appreciative if you would come over here and have a talk with Madame Li Chen. It's insurance. I don't see what else it can be."

"More than half of the things weren't the Li Chens'," said Mannering. "Most that were theirs had comparatively little value. And I can't see Raymond Li Chen carrying out that act of vandalism for money. He loved the art treasures passionately. He had a feeling for them which it's impossible to explain, but if you feel like that you don't destroy them for the sake of insurance. You told me he was wealthy——"

"Several times a millionaire," said Brabazon. "Well, what did they do it for?"

"All I know is that it must have been for a very powerful reason. It would have been like a sacrifice of everything precious to them."

"That's the kind of thing which explains why I want you to talk to Madame Li Chen," said Brabazon gruffly. "I don't really know what you're talking about, but I think she probably will. Will you come over?"

183

"I'd much rather talk to her in her shop," Mannering said. "Can you arrange that?"

*   *   *

When he went into the shop, half an hour later, he was quite sure that Madame Li Chen knew that her husband and her brother-in-law were dead. It was an expression in her eyes, and the way she held her head and looked at him, as if there was nothing which could make her suffer more than she had suffered already. She watched him as he approached her where she stood by one of the showcases. Within hand's reach of her was the Ming vase which Mannering had saved from destruction.

Mannering did not go too near, but stood and watched her for what seemed a long time. No one else was in the shop, but outside there were police and military, on guard.

"Madame Li Chen," Mannering said. "I am very, very sorry."

Her lips moved. "Thank you," she said.

He could imagine that Lorna might look and behave like this if she had just learned of his death. There was much in this woman which reminded him of Lorna, and so it was easier to talk to her than it might have been.

"There is a theory that your husband and his brother committed these acts because of the money they would receive from insurance," Mannering said. "It is a common belief."

"Do you believe it?" Madame Li Chen asked.

"No," answered Mannering flatly. "There is money, and there are treasures like those in the galleries, and they do not mean the same thing."

The woman smiled, but sombrely.

"That is what Raymond always said," she told him. "That you are one of the few men who feel towards old and beautiful things as if they were of flesh and blood, and as if they still hold the life of the past in them. They are so real to you. And they were so real to him. In those treasures there was the history of his country, the legacy of four thousand years. That

184

became more to him than money—it even became more than life."

"Why did he try to destroy so much that he loved?" Mannering asked gently.

Madame Li Chen answered quietly and without passion, but it was obvious that all the words caused her pain; yet she did not falter.

"He destroyed them because he believed that it might help to re-unite his country," she said. "He was British, and was very loyal to Britain, but his true country was China. He saw two Chinas, always at war, hating one another, setting brother against brother and family against family. He believed passionately that they should find some way of re-uniting, and he learned that all of these beautiful things were being brought from China by thieves and bandits, more and more of them, many without the knowledge of Peking or Formosa. Some were sold, some were allowed to be smuggled across the border because Peking is in such need of currency from the outside world, but the whole of Chinese culture was being ravaged. It was bad enough that many were sold to Americans; it was worse because both the government in Peking and that in Formosa were selling these treasures. To Raymond, neither was true to China, they were deliberately selling the culture of the centuries. So it was that Raymond realised for four years he had aided and abetted both, making the situation worse, by buying these goods, by storing them for Americans, by using British territory as a repository for them.

"For year after year he brooded about this. It was this deep reflection which made him feel so desperately that the two Chinas must come together, and that to salve his own conscience he must try to do that. He believed that some great shock was needed, something which was not political, not military, not commercial. And he believed that if he collected everything he could, everything he owned and all he held in trust, and then destroyed it, he could make both governments understand the wickedness of what they are doing.

"I thought he was wrong. I pleaded with him not to do these

185

things, but he believed it was the only way, and his brother believed that, also. I was Raymond's wife, and so I kept silent." After a while, she went on in a voice which Mannering could only just hear: "I think I am not sure whether he was wrong. I am not sure whether I disagreed with him because I thought it wrong, or because I knew that it would lead him to his death. I only know that I tried to prevent him, with the help of my own brothers, my own family."

She took a photograph from the show case, and handed it to Mannering. It was the man who had questioned him at the hotel, and whose description he had given to the police.

"That is my eldest brother," she said. "He is one of seven, and there are relatives of my family in many parts of the world, tied to me by blood. Please listen, Mr. Mannering, and try to understand."

24

THE STORY OF MADAME LI CHEN

MANNERING stood near the airport building, two days later, and saw the B.O.A.C. jet coming in, bright against the azure sky, brighter against the range of hills beyond the airport, hills which were in the China ruled from Peking. He pretended that he could see Lorna at one of the windows, but of course that was nonsense; but she was third to come off the plane, and he had special dispensation to go straight towards her, and not to wait for any formalities. She saw him at once, and almost broke into a run; then she checked herself. He checked himself, too, and they were half laughing when they met.

They hugged each other as if they had been parted for years.

"Yes, it's all over," Mannering told her when they were in the car put at their disposal by the Governor for the duration of their stay in Hong Kong. "I told you most of it over the telephone, and there's a whole edition of the *Tiger Standard* devoted to it, and to what the Li Chens tried to do. It doesn't come down on the side of whether it was worth trying or not, it simply hopes that it might do something to bring the two parts of China together."

"Do you think it will?" asked Lorna.

"I wouldn't like to have even an opinion about politics," said Mannering. "But I don't think that the General and the Doctor hate each other very much. It's probably like so many other things, a single step forward, an opening of the eyes, and the mind to a common cause. A quite remarkable thing has happened since I phoned you, though."

"What's that?" asked Lorna. She was looking about her at the fascinating streets, and Mannering knew just how much they would appeal to her. He was anxious to be able to give her an easy mind, so as to look about her without anxiety, and to revel in this magic island. So he said: "Listen to me now, and you won't have to concentrate on it again. The Americans who owned most of the treasures, some galleries, some big foundations, some individuals, are leaving them here in Hong Kong, on permanent loan. In one or two cases wealthy foundations are buying them from private owners, but nearly everyone is giving up something. The collection is to be housed in the Ho Sun Galleries, which will be given by the Ho Sun Trust and the Colony to another Trust, with Trustees being British, American, and Chinese, with representatives from Hong Kong territory, Peking, and Formosa. We can't ask for much more."

Lorna had almost forgotten everything around her, except what Mannering said.

"Then it has done some good already, John, that's wonderful. It's almost unbelievable!"

Mannering grinned.

"Everyone agrees that it's unbelievable, but the new Trust is actually being formed. I believe it will work, and the galleries will be a permanent memorial to the Li Chen brothers as well as to Ho Sun himself."

After a moment, Lorna said: "There's one thing I simply can't understand. Why were there such efforts to keep you away? Why were the invitations cancelled? Wouldn't it have been better if collectors and dealers from all over the world had been at the exhibition, giving it more impact everywhere?"

"That was what Madame Li Chen was afraid of," Mannering said.

"Raymond's *wife*?"

"Yes," said Mannering. "And she told me her story. She believed that Raymond meant precisely that. He meant to set the galleries on fire during the reception, to make a human sacrifice as well as to sacrifice all the artistic treasures there. So *she* cancelled the invitations, she arranged the burglaries and raids to make men like Christiansen and Vansitter rush back home. She thought that if no one from overseas was here he would not go on with what he planned. She was his wife and could not betray him, but she could create the conditions which would make it almost certain that he would be stopped!

"There was another factor—she believed that someone knew what her husband was really doing. She knew there had been police inquiries, and she knew I was an investigator at times. She sent the two men to Quinns—the old man was her uncle, the young one her cousin. He is still awaiting trial—I had a letter from Bristow today."

"Never mind Bristow," Lorna said impatiently. "Go on."

"When they could not keep me away Madame Li Chen concluded that I was coming to investigate. At all costs she wanted to make sure I didn't get to the exhibition—even by preventing it from opening. She and her relatives made the attempt to poison Charles Li Chen, preferring to murder an old man with little of life left, to betraying Raymond—and they hoped a murder on board would force the authorities to forbid the exhibition. They killed the little man who was caught on the aircraft-carrier because they feared he would talk. They attacked me in the hotel, and later fired at me in

188

the street, still trying to force the authorities to call the exhibition off."

Mannering paused.

The car turned a corner, and the street would have led to the Li Chen Galleries on their triangular site, but he did not direct it there.

"The fire started before the reception, surely," Lorna objected. "Wouldn't he have got what he wanted if he had waited until the Governor and all the official party was at the opening reception?"

"Yes, and he meant to do that," said Mannering. "But Madame Li Chen knew that the pencils in the catalogues were incendiary, which would explode on contact during the reception. She had to make sure that didn't happen, and she fitted a tiny timing device in one of the pencils, to go off earlier than they planned. We know what happened. We know that she was almost sure what her husband and her brother-in-law would do. She had done everything, even trying again and again to kill me. Finally, she made her own sacrifice to prevent the wholesale slaughter."

They were silent for a long time.

They said nothing of importance until they reached the hotel. Mannering took Lorna up to the room on the seventh floor, his own room with that magnificent view, led her to the window, and watched her face as she looked out. A kind of wonder dawned in her eyes, and she stared at the beauty of the scene for a long time.

Then she turned to look at Mannering.

"And we nearly decided that you wouldn't come. What a dreadful thing that would have been," she said.